# GIRL RUNNING, BOY FALLING

*Girl Running, Boy Falling*

© Kate Gordon, 2018

Published by Rhiza Edge,
An Imprint of Rhiza Press
PO BOX 1519
Capalaba QLD 4157
Australia
www.rhizaedge.com.au

Cover Design by Rhiza Press
Layout by Rhiza Press

ISBN: 9781925563528

A catalogue record for this book is available from the National Library of Australia

# GIRL RUNNING, BOY FALLING

## KATE GORDON

# PROLOGUE

The sky is butter, gold, a dream.

We sit on Grandma T's backstep eating warm ginger cake, fingers sticky and shining. The sun is lying down to rest on Grandma T's chook shed and we have dirt on our bare feet. Dirt on our fingernails too, and Wally has mud like war paint on both his cheeks.

I haven't told him. I like it.

'I'm buggered, Champ,' he says, stretching his brown arms above his head.

'You're weak,' I tell him, and he elbows me in the side.

'I'm too tired to think of a witty retort.'

'Weak and lacking in imagination.'

He growls at me, then laughs, and I am full of infinitude. Because this is us. This is me and Wally and dirty fingernails and chooks clucking and Grandma T pottering about in the kitchen.

This is sky and summer and freedom. This is everything.

'Fine then. Witty retort.' His eyes search the sky. He looks back down, smirking; clears his throat. 'How's this?' And then he goes and quotes TS Eliot—a poem about time and memories and exhaustion and transformation. 'TS Eliot,

Champ,' he says. 'How'd you like them apples?'

And this is why. This is *why*. Because of the brown eyes and the football hero status. But also—*more*—because he can quote TS Eliot, just like that.

'Eh,' I say, because I'm good at feigning casual, 'I'll pay it. You know he left his mentally-ill wife to be locked up in an asylum and never visited her.'

'Harsh,' Wally whispers, exhaling. We sit in silence for a perfect moment.

Wally leans over and picks a leaf from the kaffir lime tree we just helped Grandma T pot. He holds it to his nose and inhales. 'Wow,' he says. 'Here. Smell it.' He passes it to me. 'We should make a curry together out of this.'

'I'm not too good at curries,' I admit. 'I'm better at baking. Maybe I could make a kaffir lime syrup cake, or a kaffir lime and coconut pudding?'

I take the leaf and hold it to my nose. It smells like this day; it smells like the endless sky.

'Ahhh, Champ,' Wally says, like he knows my thoughts. 'Do you ever look at the sky and think that's where we belong? Like maybe the world is the wrong way around and we're meant to be up there, floating?'

If Peter were here, or Melody, they'd laugh at Wally for saying such a crooked thing. If Peter or Melody were here, Wally wouldn't have said it at all. He only ever talks like this with me. And I always answer him seriously.

With the others—with everyone else—Wally is the tough Nick Wallace: the joker, the footy player, the coolest kid in school.

With me he's soft as that leaf and he talks in poems. So I

must be a bit special, right?

'I like being on the ground,' I admit to him. 'I like having my feet somewhere stable. Up in the sky, you've got nothing holding you. You'd never be home.'

Wally doesn't reply to that. He looks away, squinting into the sun. I worry that I've said something stupid. Again.

'It's because I'm boring, I know,' I say. 'Because you're the sort of person who flies and I'm just me, stuck down here with her feet on the ground.'

'No,' he says, shaking his head. 'It's better, being like you. You're solid. You'd never float away.'

'Tiger!' Grandma T calls out. Wally suppresses a smirk, the way he always does when Grandma T or Auntie Kath call me *that* name.

Even though it's my proper name. Even though it's the name I've been called the longest, years before teachers called me 'Therese', Wally called me 'Champ', or anyone ever called me 'Resey'. I have lots of names because I am lots of things.

So many different pieces. As many pieces as there are leaves in this garden.

I'm the girl who goes to school; the girl who works at Woolies. I'm the girl with the lead role in the college musical. I'm the girl who plays lead clarinet in the senior concert band. I'm the girl who likes to read poetry. I'm the friend. I'm the canteen volunteer. I'm the footy fan; the baker; the niece.

I'm the girl who writes letters to someone who never returns them. I send away all my thoughts and memories— *every piece of me.*

And she never writes back.

Somewhere, far away, she takes the pieces and she makes

them into a picture of who she thinks I am. I wonder if it looks anything like me.

I wonder how shit all my pieces must look to her. They must because she never writes back.

'Coming, Grandma T!' I call out.

Wally stands and offers me his hand, I take it and we walk to the kitchen, our fingers still laced together.

And I would soar into the sky with him. I would.

But he drops my hand when we walk inside, and starts talking to Grandma T about footy. If you didn't know any better—if you were just watching from the outside, you'd think everything is normal.

Just a girl and her best friend and her grandma and sandwiches on a summer's day.

You'd have to look really hard to notice that everything is broken.

Hi Dad,

See me running?

See how high I can jump to catch the ball?

See me reach for the stars.

See me jump over the moon.

Maybe, if I jump high enough, I'll jump all the way to you.

# CHAPTER ONE

'Are you going to eat that?'

Peter is lolled on the desiccated grass. His ears are pink from the late winter sun. 'You're getting burned,' I say.

'It's just the hair,' he laments, patting his bushfire curls. 'The curse of the ranga. You always look a little bit pink from the reflection or something. Whatever. I'm bloody hungry, though.'

He eyes the other half of my Vegemite sandwich. I squish it to bite-sized and push it into my mouth.

'You're a pig.'

'You've already eaten two sausage rolls!' I say it through a mouthful of sandwich. 'Not getting any of this!'

'You're disgusting, Resey,' Peter groans. 'And mean.' He turns his face back to the sun.

A thump beside me announces Melody's arrival. 'You're burnt,' she says to Peter.

'What is it with you girls? I'm going to tan and then I'll look just like one of those blokes off *Home and Away* and all the footy groupies will be begging for my sweet, sweet love.'

Melody tuts. 'Someday soon, Peter, we are going to have a big talk about your obsession with the Grade Nine footy groupies. I'm sure there's something Freudian going on there.

Make a time to have a chat, okay?' Peter shakes his head and closes his eyes again. Melody digs into her backpack and pulls out a foil-wrapped parcel. She passes it over. 'From Mum.'

I take it gratefully. Mrs Kwong is the best cook in town.

'She reckons you're fading away to a shadow.'

I roll my eyes. 'Unless Chinese shadows look much rounder than Aussie ones, she's dreaming.'

Melody sighs. 'Mum shows love through food. It's pathological.'

'And yet you're still a supermodel.' I'm not exaggerating. My best friend is greyhound-thin with legs that stretch for miles. Melody Kwong is the girl in the dreams of all the boys in town. Shame she's not into boys. And all the other girls-who-are-into-girls are too scared to approach her because she's heaven and they're worried she'll break their fragile hearts.

Melody doesn't care anyway. She doesn't want to fall in love. She thinks there's something deeply psychologically wrong with those who do. She doesn't believe in kindred spirits and she doesn't believe in monogamy, and yet she's been *my* soulmate ever since we first met.

Melody and I have been best mates since Grade One. She thumped down beside me on a tree stump where I'd been sitting, alone and terrified. 'Melody Kwong,' she said, holding out her hand. 'You look depressed. But don't worry. I'm going to be a psychologist when I'm grown up. I can fix you.'

And she took me home that night to meet her mum, who was dressed like a rock star, and dancing in the kitchen to hip hop, while baking cupcakes. Melody introduced me as 'my new bestie, Resey Geeves. She has problems. But don't worry. I'm on the case.'

And her mum said, 'Call me Lexi,' and then, 'You're too skinny, Resey Geeves.' And she gave me my first ever dumpling. I told her that my auntie liked to make oven chips and cornflakes, and that sometimes we had cups of tea and Cheezels instead of dinner. When Auntie Kath came to pick me up, Lexi took her by the hand, looked deep into her eyes and said, 'You, my girl, need to learn how to cook.'

Ten years on, Auntie Kath is still trying.

I bite into the pork bun. It tastes like a thousand little sparkles of something other and wonderful. Nobody knows exactly what Lexi puts in her pork buns. She won't tell anyone, not even her daughter.

Melody pulls a dead dandelion from the ground and rubs it on Peter's nose. 'Where's Wally?' she asks.

'Footy,' Peter says, lifting a shoulder and dropping it lazily back down. He swipes the dandelion and twirls it slowly between his fingers. 'Where I should be. Team doesn't know what it's missing out on.' He says this even though we all know Peter sucks at footy. But he keeps trying for the team every year. He's determined to make it someday.

'You should give up on the football thing, Peetles,' Melody drawls. 'Find a new hobby. Hey! Maybe you should take up ballet instead. You'd look so cute in a little tutu.' She reaches out and tickles Peter on the ribs.

Instead of punching her on the bicep, which is what I expect, Peter looks at Melody, sternly. 'Nothing wrong with blokes wearing dresses.'

'I'm the last person to say there was,' Mel replies, crossing her arms.

'Good. Glad to hear it.' A thoughtful expression takes

over Peter's face. 'Hey … lots of chicks do ballet, don't they? Hardly any blokes. Maybe I should get myself some tights …'

Now, that's more like the Peter we know and love (despite his façade of misogyny, which, obviously, we never let him get away with).

'Seriously, though, Peter.' Melody's wearing her therapist face now, her fingers steepled and her brows knitted. 'We will talk.'

'Right.' Peter sighs. 'I look forward to that.'

'What would you do without me?' Melody asks, shaking her head and stretching her long limbs under the sun that seems to shine just for her. 'You'd both be emotional messes. Peter with his pretence of being a sexist pervert—which we all know is all a deeply-and-embarrassingly misguided attempt at self-preservation. You, with …' She grins at me, wickedly. I feel my cheeks burn. I shoot her a don't-mention-his-name look. Peter doesn't know how I feel about Wally. Because he is a clueless male. Which is usually annoying but, in this case, is completely useful. I don't want him to know. He'd be all awkward about it, and the whole thing is awkward enough as it is.

'So,' Melody says, sweetly. 'How are our beloved Hawks, Peter?'

Relief is in front of me, dancing in the air like a pink winged piglet.

'Hawks are on track,' Peter says. 'The North Hobart match last weekend was a blip. It was an "away" game and it was bad weather.'

'I remember,' Melody grumbles. 'Even my undies were soaked.' She turns to me. 'Tell me why I go with you again? I don't even like football.'

'Would you prefer it if we went to the women's league matches, instead?' I ask, glaring at her.

Melody rolls her eyes. 'Well, that would be better. Something to look at, at least.'

'Perving on all the girls in their footy uniforms?' Peter says, grinning. 'Hot.'

Melody crosses her impossible legs and clasps her slender hands around her knees. She leans forward. 'You know, Peter, your preoccupation with my attractions is clearly an indication of your pathological obsession with me. And, since I will never be yours, it speaks loudly of deep-seeded attachment issues. Tell me, did your parents practise controlled crying when you were a baby?'

'Huh?' Peter looks at me in confusion. I shrug. I have no idea what she's talking about, either.

'Were you breastfed?' Melody goes on.

'Yuck!' Peter shakes his head and plugs in his headphones, studiously ignoring us. 'Bloody girls,' he mutters before he loses himself in the Triple J lunch show.

Melody turns back to me, smiling smugly. She knows she's won and Melody loves winning. Especially against Peter. 'What were we talking about? Oh, right. Footy girls. Nope. Any girl who actually likes that Neanderthal sport—sorry, Resey, but you know it's not my style. Dancing, though … I've been watching dance documentaries on YouTube and … oh, Resey, take me to a jazz ballet concert any day of the week and I'd be in heaven. Does that make me sound pervy? Like Peter?' She sticks her hands out, flat-palmed, and wiggles them. 'It's just that I've discovered I have a *thing* for jazz hands.'

I try a laugh, but I know it sounds false.

Melody drops her hands and sighs. 'Resey, what is your problem? It's Wallace, isn't it? It's never anything but bloody Wallace.'

Of course it is. It will always be Wally.

'I saw him come up to you after the game,' Melody says.

I blush at the memory. Wally always heads straight for me after the game. I'm always the person he wants to talk to first.

'He likes your baking,' Melody hisses. 'I hate to say it, Resey, but it's your scones he's after. And that's not a metaphor.'

She lies back down in the sun. More loudly, she declares, 'Besides, the scout's going to come to a match any day now, and they'll draft Wally, and then he'll be off to the mainland and gone forever.'

Peter's taken his headphones out. 'You'd better believe it,' he says and stares up at the clouds. 'Some people are just born lucky, aren't they, Resey?'

# CHAPTER TWO

Melody and Peter are bickering, as usual. It's the normal stuff: Peter has to stop pretending to be a complete arsehole because some people actually believe him and, after the Me Too movement, there's no excuse for even pretending to be a creepy letch. Melody has to stop trying to convert everybody because sometimes people don't want to live inside a feminism echo-chamber. All is usual in the lunch spot. I'm trying to tune them out. I have the new Rainbow Rowell book—a present from Auntie Kath—and I'm trying to find a spare moment to squeeze in a couple of paragraphs before the bell rings for third period.

Except, as always, Melody won't let me be. She wants me to talk.

'I'm sure Resey would be an activist too,' she says. 'If she had the time.' She looks at me meaningfully.

'I know,' I mutter, before she can say it, '*I do too much.*'

'It isn't healthy,' Melody says, grabbing a chunk of her long dark hair and plaiting it loosely. 'You're young, Resey. You're meant to be a menace to society. You're meant to be having fun and causing chaos, before you have to put on that suit and make, like, Powerpoint presentations. Stop trying to be old, Resey. Stop scheduling every second. It's harmful to your development. Be terrifying! Teenagers are meant to be *terrifying*!' Melody secures her hair with a scrunchie from her wrist and regards me, one eyebrow raised. 'How else are we going to fix the world?'

'Monologue over?' I ask, looking pointedly back down at my book.

'Not even,' Melody replies. 'I could go on forever about the psychological implications of your passivity and your micro-managed life. Where should I start?'

I sigh. I really don't want to get into another conversation about how I use extra-curricular activities as an 'avoidance strategy'. This is another of Melody's theories. She thinks I make my life busy so I don't have to think about 'the bad stuff'. By which she means my mum and dad.

'I mean, when did you last come with us to the plaza after school?'

'I'm—'

'Busy,' Melody finishes for me, and I can't argue, because that's exactly what I was going to say. And I feel terrible. I'm a terrible friend.

I am too many things and too many pieces and the friend bit of me is broken.

'I'll come today?' I say, sheepishly. 'There's concert band practice on after school but I don't have to be there. They're working on pieces from the musical, and I'm in the acting cast, so I don't need to learn them. I was only going to practise to help out with the Grade Sevens and Eights.'

'You're freaking Mary Poppins,' Melody groans.

'Shut up. I said I'd come shopping.'

'Most excellent,' Melody says, grinning. 'I'll let Roz know. We'll hit the shops, like *bam*.'

Just then, as if hearing her name summoned her, the auburn head of our other best mate, Roz, appears in the distance.

And at her side is Wally.

My belly flips. Pork bun, Vegemite sandwich and all.

His curls are wet from the showers and so is the top of his school shirt. He looks exhausted. I wish I'd saved half of my pork bun to give him.

I wish I had anything to give him. I wish I'd thought to bring the scones I made last night. Melody's right, of course. Wally does love my scones.

Roz gets to us first. She skips, jumps, then flops in front of Melody. 'You're late,' says Mel.

'Double chemistry.' Roz is literally the only person I know who is made happy by extra science class. 'I am so close to a break-through. It's killing me. I just can't get the temperature right. But I will get there if it kills me.'

'I thought it already was killing you,' Mel says.

'What?' Roz scrunches up her freckly nose.

'You're still in Chemistry Land, aren't you?' sighs Melody.

'I am still in Chemistry Land,' Roz concedes, with a grin. Her gingery eyebrows shoot up. 'Ooh!' she says. 'Oobleck!' She reaches into her bag and pulls out a notebook with a picture of Albert Einstein on it.

'Huh?' says Mel. When Roz doesn't reply, she gives up. 'Wallace, my man!' she calls out. 'You got chewy on your boots? Hurry the hell up.'

Wally sits down by my side. 'Keep your shirt on, Kwong,'

he says, chucking a piece of wadded-up notebook paper at her head. 'I'm thinking about very deep things.'

'You have low blood sugar,' Melody says. 'Clearly.'

'I don't have any treats for you today, I'm afraid, Wally,' I tell him.

Wally laughs and slings his arm around my shoulder. 'You know it's a treat just to see you, Resey. I mean, but your cooking *is*, like, the meaning of life …'

I catch sight of Melody narrowing her eyes. I ignore her. 'You're an idiot, Wally,' I say.

'Are you serious?' he says. 'About no treats? Not even one bickie?'

I shake my head.

'FML,' he groans.

'You know, nobody says that out loud, right?' I tell him.

'What would I do without you,' he says, 'to stop me from being a total dork?'

'You … would be a total dork?'

'True that,' he says. 'Unfortunately, completely true.'

Later, as we walk back to class, Melody leans in and asks, 'Do you want to talk about it?'

I shake my head. 'No thanks, Mel.'

I don't want to talk about it. What's the point of talking about any of it? All the talking in the world wouldn't change the fact that this situation is *incontrovertibly* shit.

Because all I want to do is kiss him, and he doesn't have a clue. He would never have a clue. Because if Nick Wallace ever knew that I loved him, then I'd lose my best friend.

Dear Dad,

I keep trying to ...

I just want to say ...

I need you to know ...

Why can't I bloody talk to you?

I need to bloody talk to you.

I need someone to bloody listen.

Hear me.

Hear me.

# CHAPTER THREE

My mum was born here—in this town, in this house, on this tiny island, down the bottom of the big one.

My grandparents didn't plan it that way. Grandma T is not a hippy, even though she's spent time in an ashram in Marrakech. She's a biologist, an atheist, a pragmatist. She went to Marrakech to research a project for her science degree.

She thought the chanting was claptrap and fell asleep in meditation.

Grandma T was booked into the hospital up the hill. The doctors thought it might have to be a caesarean because my mum was upside-down.

'Always heading off in the wrong direction,' Grandma T says about Mum. 'But you couldn't tell her. Never could make that girl go where you wanted her to. Always moving, moving, moving, along whichever path she damn well wanted to move along.'

They were hoping she'd turn. Much as she respected medicine, Grandma T knew that caesareans were hard. With a natural birth, it might hurt like hell for a good while, but then a lovely rush of hormones makes you forget all that.

The hormones help your milk come in and the baby pops out wanting it.

With a caesarean, you don't feel as much at first, since you're numbed. But you sure feel it after, and for longer. You don't get the hormones, so making milk is harder. And you're weak; so weak and sore you can't hold your baby, sometimes for a month or more.

Grandma T was really keen on her baby turning around.

She was making relish when Mum decided she wanted to be in the world.

Grandma T makes amazing relish—it's her one concession to 'being old and born during the war'. She makes incredible sponges too, and ginger cakes, but she does it in secret and mostly eats them herself. She only lets me have a slice, sometimes, because she knows I inherited her love of cake. I had to pinkie swear when I was five not to tell *anyone* that she's a closeted Nigella Lawson.

She lets Wally have as many slices as he wants, though, because she thinks he's a prince. Because he helps with the horses and watches *Doctor Who* with her and laughs at her jokes and tells her she's 'cool'.

She *is* cool. She's definitely not an ordinary grandmother.

And she does make a mean relish.

And so she was making it the day her baby decided to turn the right way and push herself out into the world.

'The one day that girl was heading in the right direction,' Grandma T says, 'but it was at the wrong time.'

Auntie Kath remembers the glass bowl hitting the tiles, tomatoes painting the kitchen red and the wooden spoon clattering after it. She remembers the bellow, 'like one of the cows in Bob's paddock over the road'.

She remembers Grandma T screaming, 'Get your father, Kathlynn. Get him bloody *right now*.'

She remembers water all over the floor and thinking it must have come from the pot on the stove, until she saw it was all over Grandma's bottom as well.

'Is she coming?' she asked.

Grandma T nodded. 'She's on her way. Now get your father.'

Granda Craig was down at the dam, in his wide-brimmed leather hat and gumboots, looking for 'a blocked something, or a flooded something else'—Auntie Kath can't remember and neither can Granda Craig.

All they remember is the moment Aunt Kath said: 'Mum's got water all over her and she's mooing like a cow.'

Granda Craig scooped bare-footed Kathlynn up into his arms and they ran together through the mud and past the prancing horses and back to the house that smelled like tomatoes.

And they heard it. A new bellowing. Not like a cow, this one—more like an oystercatcher in a particularly bad temper.

Mum was already there.

'Slipped out like a little baby bird,' Grandma T said, before she fainted.

The ambulance came and took Grandma T and her baby to the hospital. They put my mum in a special crib, with extra air, and put a tube in her tummy because she didn't have the skills yet to drink from Grandma.

When Grandma T was taken down to see her baby, she told Granda Craig that Mum needed a nature name 'since you were down the paddock when she came'.

Her name was Laurel. But they called her Birdie.

Auntie Kath says she knew, in that moment, that my mother would be the wild one—the flying one—and it was up to her to be the one who stayed on the ground.

When I was little, I used to say to her, 'I never want to be a flying thing, like she is. I want to stay on the ground with you.'

# CHAPTER FOUR

We're sitting at Banjo's: Roz and Melody and me in our favourite booth. Melody is dismantling a sausage roll. She eats the pastry first—after tearing it into silk-thin strips—then breaks off tiny hunks of grey-pink sausage.

Melody eats the way she lives—picking everything apart and examining its pieces, then peeling back the layers to see what's beneath.

Roz has a large cappuccino. She is scooping up the chocolatey froth with her index finger and licking it off, the way she never would if her strict parents were here.

She's still prim, quiet and correct, because you can't change the configuration of a girl just by giving her froth and chocolate. But she's more relaxed with us. She smiles with us.

At her house, she's not allowed to wear track pants. She has to wear a skirt to dinner.

With us, she balances a spoon on her nose. Not loudly, and she goes pink when she does it, but it's something. We are her home. We're all each other's home. And we're all flawed and we all make each other furious, sometimes, but that's just like every family, isn't it?

I have an apple scroll and I'm eating it from the outside

in. I've already picked off the icing. I've kept some of it aside, to make a little sculpture—it will entertain Roz and give Melody fodder for her psychoanalysis.

Last time I made a dead mouse, belly-up on the laminex table. Melody had a field day with that.

The three of us are hemmed in by a teetering pile of bags from our shopping expedition. Melody bought a stack of *Buffy* comics and the new Haim CD. Roz bought a pair of glittery flats and a navy blue dress ('It *is* for church,' she sighed, when Melody told her it looked like a dress you'd wear to church). Roz had stared longingly at a ruby red lipstick in Priceline, but left it on the shelf, with a muttered, 'My parents would find out, somehow.'

I didn't get anything. I have enough pairs of jeans, and enough hoodies, to last me a lifetime, and a pile of books beside my bed, so high I might finish them by the time I'm forty.

'I knew you wouldn't buy anything,' Melody growls. 'You are so predictable. It's neurotic.' She pegs a piece of soggy sausage in my direction. I duck and it bounces off the glass panel behind me and into Roz's cuppa.

'Gross,' she sighs, fishing it out. She examines it and pops it in her mouth. She chews thoughtfully. 'Sausage roll is better with froth,' she decides.

Melody mimes gagging. She turns, pointedly, away from Roz. 'Anyway, why do you never buy anything, Resey? You must be loaded, since you work all those hours at the place where dreams die, and you don't spend anything. Ever.'

'That's not true. I bought that Josh Ritter CD a few weeks back,' I point out. 'And the new reed box for my clarinet and a new pair of work shoes.'

'Twenty bucks at JB, ten dollars at the Barrett's and thirty at Target.' Melody ticks them off on her fingers. 'Where do the other hundreds of dollars go?'

I shrug. 'I mean, we both donate to that school for girls in Sierra Leone—'

'Totally necessary, but not *fun.*'

'—and I spend a bit on books and art stuff too—'

Melody interrupts. 'And you never have time to read or paint!'

I ignore her.

'—but mostly it goes in the bank.'

'For what, Geeves? I mean, I'm all for female empowerment through financial freedom, but there is *time* for that. Now, you should be living it up.'

I shrug. 'I'll use it for uni or travel or … something.'

When I say 'travel', my heart thuds.

Because I want to travel. *I do.* I want to *see* that school in Sierra Leone. I want to see the Louvre, too, and the Guggenheim in Bilbao. I want to go to concerts at the Vienna State Opera or musicals on Broadway. Heck, I'd love to catch a soccer game in Manchester or Liverpool, just to see why they think their code is better than Aussie Rules.

But …

I'm scared. Of leaving. Of flying. Of letting my feet lift off the ground.

What if getting on an aeroplane is the thing that changes me? What if it's my trigger? What if it turns me into *her*?

'I don't know,' I mumble, shrugging. 'I'll figure it out.'

Melody inclines her head to one side. 'That's the point,

Resey. You don't know what you want to spend your money on. I think that's a manifestation of your inner conflict, don't you? You don't know what you want at all! You don't know if you want to be a painter or an actor or a musician or—Wally!'

'I don't want to be Wally,' I protest, my forehead furrowing. 'What are you on about?'

'No. I mean Wally's here. There.' Melody points out the back window of Banjo's, the one that looks onto the fountain in the middle of the plaza.

He's sitting, staring at the water.

My heart trembles.

He looks like a painting.

'Isn't he meant to be at practice?' Roz asks, meeting my eye.

I shrug.

But he is. Of course he is. It's the Hawks' big game against Clarence on the weekend. Wally should definitely be at training.

I narrow my eyes. He's holding something. A book, but not a book. Not a reading book, anyway. A notebook?

He's scribbling in it, furiously.

'Dunno. Maybe he's sick,' says Melody. 'But going back to what I was saying ...'

And Melody forgets Wally and returns to her favourite topic: my disordered brain.

I tune out; I watch Wally.

He seemed quiet at lunch time. But Wally can get like that. Some days, he goes inside himself. It's another thing that makes us the same.

Peter reckons he's thinking about footy, replaying marks and kicks and tackles. I think it's more than that. There's more than footy in Wally's head. It's just that I'm the only one who knows it. I'm the only one he shares it with.

There's the shape of clouds, and the sound rain makes on Grandma T's tin roof ('like a hundred thousand little heartbeats or tiny wings beating'), and what happens when we die.

Wally has this idea that heaven and hell are just a place your brain goes to in that moment when your heart stops beating. He reckons those couple of seconds stretch out into infinite years and you spend all that time reliving your life— the things you did and, more importantly, the people you loved.

The good people—the ones with lots of friends and family who loved them—remembering their lives is a joyful thing. So that's heaven. The nasty people spend eternity going over all the bad stuff they did, and knowing they never really loved anyone; they were never really loved.

That's hell.

He says that the afterlife is golden or grey and it's up to you, now, what colour it becomes.

There's more than footy in Wally's brain.

Of course, he talks about the scout, too, and the AFL, and how he'll play for any club, as long as it isn't Collingwood. He talks about the Brownlow medal and the best-and-fairest trophy and premierships and glory.

And that's what other people see. They see the boundless smile; the excitement. But when it's just us, his face changes. It clouds, and he asks what he should do if the scout doesn't love him; if the AFL doesn't want him. I reply, because I've said it before, 'You'll do maths, remember? You'll be an engineer, like your dad.'

And Wally always says, 'Maybe. Maybe I could, Champ. That would be the sensible thing to do, wouldn't it? But I'd never be as good at maths as my dad was. I'll never be as good a footy player, either, but I reckon if I tried hard enough I could do okay.'

And I think about how I'd quite like to be an actor, even though it's not the *sensible thing*.

Doing the sensible thing always makes me feel hollow inside, but at least it's not scary.

'Maybe it's good,' I tell Wally, 'to just do the thing that's okay. Maybe that's an okay thing to do.'

Wally doesn't reply, because he'll probably get what he wants. The special thing; the wild thing; not just the okay thing.

Because he's Nick Wallace.

'So, you still love him?'

'Hmm?' I drag my eyes away from Wally, sitting at the fountain. Melody has a cat-like grin on her face.

And a smear of sauce on her chin.

'What?'

'You still totally in love with Nicholas Alexander Wallace?'

*Of course. Because he tells me things he tells nobody else. Of course, because he quotes poetry, but never seems like a dick when he does it. Of course, because he's Nick Wallace.*

'Shut up.'

'Mel, drop it,' says Roz. I smile at her, gratefully. Sometimes I think Roz gets me more than I give her credit for. She smiles back. 'Do you think I should get my hair cut?' she asks, blowing on her auburn fringe so it puffs up and out of her eyes. She's trying to distract Melody.

I love her so much.

But Melody, of course, being Melody, will not be distracted.

'Resey,' says Melody. 'This Wally thing? It's starting to get pathological. She's been in love with him for, what, three years, eight months and ...'

'Melody!' I moan.

'Leave her,' Roz says, gently. 'Let's just talk about something else.'

'I love your hair,' I tell her. 'You look like Lizzie Siddal.'

'It's boring,' she sighs.

'You both suck,' says Melody. 'Shave your head, Roz. Live a little. Both of you, live a little, before you're old or dead.'

Down at the fountain, Wally stands up. He tucks the book inside his backpack, runs his hand through his curls and shakes his head like a dog drying off after a bath. He walks away towards the Mount Street exit.

'So you do still love him?' Melody won't let it drop. She's a pitt bull.

I look away from Wally's retreating back. 'Auntie Kath says that what people call love is just a chemical reaction that compels animals to breed,' I say. 'I think it's a quote from *Rick and Morty*, actually ...'

'I'm never falling in love,' says Melody, licking the top of her sauce packet. 'It's a totally unnatural state of being. Humans aren't meant to be monogamous. And besides, it just makes you *miserable.*'

'My parents are happy,' Roz says, and we both look at her in shock. The last thing we would ever imagine Roz's parents being is *happy*. 'What?' she asks, looking between us. 'They are happy with each other. It's only me who disappoints them.'

'How could you disappoint anyone?' I ask, as Melody says, 'They're only happy with each other because they're both so anal and dysfunctional. And because they've bought into the patriarchal concept of marriage for life. Which is so outdated, it's not even funny.'

'Well—' Roz begins. Melody cuts her off.

'And as for Resey and her irrational fixation on Nick Wallace, well, it has to stop. Life is short, Therese. Now, what you should do is ...'

As Melody goes on and on, picking apart my choices, my mistakes, my life, I watch Wally walk towards the exit.

He looks up, sort of in my direction, but past me, as if the two of us are in completely different realities—parallel planes of existence.

I wonder what he sees.

Dear Dad,
Have you ever noticed that
You can smell the rain before it falls?
Do you think it's like that with people?
Do you think you can smell it on them
Before they fall?

# CHAPTER FIVE

Auntie Kath drives me to work in her tiny, semi-vintage (we're talking noughties vintage) Beetle car. The fake gerbera wobbles in its little holder, as we bump along the road.

'Why don't you get rid of that thing?' I ask Kath, not for the first time. 'You hate gerberas.'

'It came with the car,' is Kath's customary answer. 'It feels wrong to get rid of it. Mabel might get sad.'

'Mabel is inanimate.'

'Don't listen to her, old girl.' Auntie Kath peers over to me, one eyebrow cocked. 'You know she's older than you are. Show her some respect.'

'Weirdo artist woman.'

Auntie Kath throws her head back and lets out a throaty laugh. 'Not weird,' she says, wiping at the edges of her black-lined eyes. 'Geez, kid. If you could see some of the jerks I went to uni with. Then you'll know weird.'

'I wonder if any of them can cook …' I say, wistfully.

'Most of them can barely remember their own names.' Kath puts two fingers up to her lips and blows out with a wink at me. I get the idea.

She turns into the Woolies car park and pulls to a smooth

stop in one of the allocated pram spots. Auntie Kath's car might be slightly eccentric, but her driving is never less than perfect.

'Off you trot,' she says, reaching over to open my door. 'Scan those Tim Tams and mini hot dogs like your life depends on it. Make this family proud.'

'Thanks for the lift, Auntie Kath.'

'Bring me home some Tim Tams? I shouldn't have mentioned them. Now my belly requires them.'

'Done.' I shut the passenger door. The gerbera wobbles and sags sideways like a tired old lady.

I watch Auntie Kath through the rear-view mirror as she sets it right again and pats Mabel's dashboard tenderly. She gives me two toots and glides off into the night.

*\*\*\**

Rhino is already in the staff room, eating a reheated steak-and-mushroom pie from the deli.

'Rhino,' I say, nodding. 'Changing it up. You haven't had steak and mushroom before.'

He looks up. His dark eyes sparkle as he grins at me. 'I'm trying all of them. I'm living dangerously. It's a little pastry-based adventure, Tiger!'

Rhino is one of the few people outside my family who calls me by my proper name. It's one of our things. His real name is Ryan, but I never call him that either.

'Hey, what do you get if you cross a tiger with a kangaroo?' he asks. I roll my eyes. Rhino has made it his vocation in life to Google the entirety of the world's tiger jokes and enrich my life by reciting them all to me.

They're getting progressively worse.

'I don't know, Rhino,' I answer. 'What do you get if you cross a tiger with a kangaroo?'

'A stripy jumper.'

I laugh despite myself. 'Actually terrible, Rhino. So, how's tricks?' I ask. It's another one of our things.

He gives his traditional reply. 'Oh, you know, Tiges. Just chillin'. Killin'.'

It's a line from a movie Rhino likes. I can't remember which one and I can't remember when I first heard him say it, or why I started saying it too. It's just one of those silly things you say when you work at the meaningless existence that is Woolworths. It's just a thing; something to share.

I pull up a chair across from him at the plastic table. 'So how is steak and mushroom?'

'Awful, Tiges. Awful. But, as I said, adventurous. How's Auntie K?'

'Vehemently insisting on her normalness.'

'"Normal" is subjective. Your Auntie Kath's version of normal is pretty awesome, you know.'

'I know, you know, I know. I'm only teasing her. Her car is pretty bizarre, though.'

'Her car is for the win.'

'You totally cannot pull off that saying.' I swipe a chunk of pastry that's dislodged itself from the rest of the pie, making a break for freedom from Rhino's ravenous mouth.

'I'm aware of that,' he says. 'But, to be fair, I don't think anybody really can.'

'Greetings, comrades.' Flo salutes us as she makes a beeline for the fridge.

Flo's real name is Chloe but somehow, over the year or

so we've all been working together at Woolies, it's become Flo. Chloe. Chlo. Chlo-flo. Flo. Now, like Ryan and Therese, Chloe also has been discarded.

'Anybody left anything good in here?'

Work has this rule that if you leave something behind after your shift and it's not labelled, it's fair game. You can get some good stuff, if you work the night shift. Day people often bring dinner leftovers for lunch, and then end up caving for Jointley's hot chips instead. This place can make hot chips seem like a necessity.

'Nup.' Flo sighs, slamming the door. 'Only some of Grant's half-eaten korma. And we all know that stuff's the coconut-flavoured antichrist.' She shudders. 'I still bear the emotional scars.'

Flo flops glumly on the chair beside Rhino and ferrets around in her handbag, pulling out a foil-wrapped parcel. 'Guess it's Mum's curried-egg sandwiches then.'

I wrinkle my nose. 'I can smell them from here.'

'You could smell them in Siberia,' Rhino adds.

'They're good.' Flo talks through a mouth of lurid yellow mush. She swallows and grins. 'And I can breathe really hard at all the men who call me "Darling". *Winning.*'

'Is Eloise on tonight?' Rhino asks, hopefully.

Eloise is our night manager. She's doing Early Childhood at uni and she treats us like we're her baby ducks. Most importantly, she turns a blind eye when we slack off and gossip.

Flo shakes her head. 'Miserably, tonight we will be subjected to the awesomeness that is—'

'Chloe Hammersmith, service twenty, register three please. Chloe Hammersmith.'

'The Jamienator,' we moan in unison.

Flo looks at her watch and sighs. 'Seriously? I'm one minute late. Far out, the Jamienator just loves the power, doesn't he? It's gone straight to his stupid, pimply propeller-head. See you guys out there.'

Flo shoves the rest of her sandwich in her mouth. 'I'm not even gunna have a Tic Tac and I'm gunna breathe straight in Jamie's stupid face.' She shakes her head. 'Bloody wanker,' she mutters as she strides out of the staff room.

Rhino pins his name badge to his tie. 'Guess we'd better go back out and do some fruit and veg cramming, if we're going to avoid the wrath of Jamie.'

'Eloise will sort him out if he has a go at us,' I say, but I'm standing already. 'Beurre Bosc pears are back and we have dragon fruit. They're code two-oh-one-six. Oh, and custard apples have made a reappearance, and Dutch creams, but I'd be double checking with the customers about those because they look exactly like—'

'Okay, okay, I get it, Tiges.' Rhino is grinning. 'You're a fresh produce Rain Man. Seriously, is there anything you're not perfect at?'

I sigh. 'No. Not really. Not that it gets me anywhere.'

'You mean your *el tragico* love life?'

I clip on my neck scarf. 'Among other things.'

I don't mind talking about love with Rhino. I don't mind talking about anything with Rhino. We may not talk about clouds and death and the future, but when I talk to Rhino nothing feels serious. Even my non-existent love life seems somehow kind of funny. It feels as if we're laughing at ourselves. At our misery. We're in this together.

Rhino—with his big nose and his braces and his wild long black hair—is like me. We're messy people. Lost people. Rhino understands.

He knows what I'm talking about, when I say that my heart is like a tomato that's been trampled by a marauding bull in Pamplona (at one of those festivals where dickhead Australians line up to get gored).

Rhino had a girlfriend, a while back. Her name was Aysha. She was horrible to him and broke his poor little rhinoceros heart. There were no tiger jokes for a whole week.

Rhino knows love; the wrong kind. The kind that hurts.

He hasn't mentioned a girl for a while now. I wonder if he's got his eye on anyone. I feel bad that I haven't asked him.

'What about you?' I ask. 'Are you *truly, madly, deeply* in love with anyone?'

'Excellent daggy nineties reference, Tiger,' he says. 'Savage Garden, I do believe. Whatever happened to them?'

'You didn't answer my question, Rhizencrantz.' I pull his long black ponytail. 'Are you under love's heavy burden?'

Rhino gives a small salute. 'Since you asked so creatively ... I am, in fact, a rhino in love.'

I punch him on the arm. 'You have a girlfriend? That's great! But why did I not know this?'

Rhino looks past me. 'Um, I'm a man of mystery?' he says. He waggles his eyebrows at me.

I clap my hands. 'Ee! I must know everything. Tell me all about your girlfriend. What's her name? What's she—'

'No time, Tiger,' Rhino says. 'You know the Jamienator waits for no man. Or tiger. Or rhinoceros.'

'I know,' I sigh. 'Remember last time we were late?'

'Toothbrushes. Potato crates. Scrubbing. *I remember.*' He rolls his eyes. 'The man is a walking bundle of fun. All those hours of *World of Warcraft* have certainly given our fearless wiener both compassion and a sense of humour. Lucky, we have each other. And Flo.'

'Yeah,' I say. 'Thank heavens for that. What would I do without you, Rhino?'

'Shrivel up like a sultana, I should imagine,' he replies.

'My life was a gaping hole before you, my ungulate friend,' I say, linking my arm through his as we walk towards the service desk.

'I know it,' he replies. And then, he begins to hum. I suppress a smile. This is another one of our 'things'—the humming game. Rhino loves nineties pop music. I know for a fact he knows exactly what Savage Garden are up to these days. And that he knows every word to every one of their songs.

He's made this one easy for me, because we were just talking about the cheesy Australian duo moments before. '"I Knew I Loved You",' I tell him, smugly.

'*You know you did,*' he replies, winking.

We raise our voices and sing together.

And it might be sugary and bubblegum and all things bad about music, but it's a song about missing pieces and soulmates. I can't help thinking about Wally. And I feel warm inside.

Dear Dad,
There's a hole in every wall, in every chair,
in every floor,
And when I try to sit, I fall.
When I try to stand, I stumble.
When I try to find something to lean on,
I tumble.
But never all the way back to you.
Which is all I ever want—
To fall all the way back to where you are.

# CHAPTER SIX

My mum met my dad at primary school. He liked trucks and she was good at drawing them. She was good at drawing everything, actually (artistic talent runs in our family), but trucks were her speciality. She had him at, 'So, I drew this Mack Trident, right?'

'Axle forward or axle back?' he squeaked, and she knew he was hers for life.

They spent every lunch hour together, drawing and playing with my dad's Tonkas. He told her he was going to be a truckie when he was big. She knew that his mum and dad would never let him. His parents were fancy people. They lived on College Road; were best friends with Roz's grandparents. To them, she was Laurel instead of Birdie. They made her take off her shoes before she came inside. They made her wash her hands and her knees before tea (which she thought was bizarre, because she didn't eat with her knees). They muttered to each other about 'compost smells'.

Mum knew that my dad would never end up a truckie, and she was right.

My mum and dad didn't only share a love of oversized

motor vehicles. They had a unicorn, called Fiona, who lived in Grandma T's chook shed and ate all the square eggs before she and my dad could find them. Fiona laid glittery ones of her own, in exchange for the square ones, with baby unicorns inside. Sometimes Mum and Dad caught a glimpse of them—sparkling in the shards of sunlight that pierced the shed walls—before the elves came to take them away.

She and my dad would lay in wait for the elves. They wanted to follow them to the Otherwhere, where the elves lived, and where Fiona's family lived, too. And where the sprites ran to, when they were done dancing in the dam.

But the elves were too quick and wily. They knew they were being watched. They paid the chooks in special, chocolate-flavoured feed, to act as diversions, so they could run away unnoticed. And so the chooks would flap their wings, the roosters would crow, and my mum and dad would become distracted, just for a moment, and the elves would be gone.

They'd traipse back to Grandma T's, disheartened, and tell Auntie Kath all about it—the unicorns and the elves and the glittery eggs and the double-crossing chooks. Auntie Kath would draw pictures of the elves and the eggs—her pictures were beautiful, but Mum told her that they didn't look right.

So Auntie Kath would tell Mum to draw her own pictures, so she could see where she had gone wrong.

My mum and dad would take out their notebooks and their boxes of pencils to draw Fiona, the elves and sometimes the Otherwhere.

Neither of them could draw like Auntie Kath, but there was no denying that they were committed, wholeheartedly, to their Otherworld vision.

Even if my dad's drawings always had trucks in them.

Grandma T would bring them glasses of blackcurrant juice and ginger cake, hot from the oven, with butter spread on half-a-centimetre thick.

They'd all sit together—Mum, Dad, Auntie Kath and Grandma T—until the black BMW pulled up on the road (never in the driveway) and honked its horn.

'And your dad would always say, "Thanks for the cake and thanks for the juice and I'll be back tomorrow, Birdie. We'll catch those dorky elves."'

Auntie Kath's eyes look faraway and soft, when she speaks of those times. I know she can see it, inside her head, like a movie that's always playing; a constant spool of light and sound—and *her*.

She smiles. 'And Birdie would say, "Thank you for the drawing," because he would have given her his picture to keep, like he always did. And your Grandma T would say, "Look forward to seeing you tomorrow, young man. You have good dreams tonight." And, I'll never forget this, your father always looked sad then and said, "I don't think I dream." The Beemer would honk again—they never came in—and he always walked out so … diminished. When he was hunting elves and drawing trucks, your dad seemed like a tall boy, but when that black car beeped he shrank. We used to watch him walking towards it and wish we could keep him.'

They couldn't keep him. I couldn't keep him, either.

Now, Wally and I are the ones sitting together, watching the chook shed. We never see unicorns or the sneaky elves. But with Wally, I can believe that they're real.

Nick Wallace is the kind of kid who makes you believe in miracles.

'Your mum was like that, too,' Auntie Kath tells me.

And she hands me a picture she drew, while we chatted about the olden days.

It's of an elf, of course, on a unicorn. But it looks just like me. 'I'm not an elf,' I tell her. 'I'm not magical.'

She rolls her eyes and holds out her hand. 'Dance with me, Tiger.'

'There's no music playing,' I argue. 'And don't say something cheesy about dancing to the music inside my head.'

'Never,' she growls in reply. 'Would I ever say something like that? Does anyone ever say something like that, outside of American romcoms?'

'I don't think American romcoms have been a thing for at least a decade,' I point out.

Auntie Kath presses play on the old CD player that sits on top of the fridge. 'And neither have CDs,' I add.

She laughs as the first few bars of a song begin to waft out of the dusty speakers. It's a song I know well, because Auntie Kath plays it all the time. It's a song from her childhood—a song about magic and miracles from the old hippie band, Fleetwood Mac.

'Good call,' I tell her, as she skips with me around the room. 'Did you have that queued up, ready to go?'

'Nope,' she says. 'It's just magic.'

'And there are elves in Grandma T's shed,' I drawl.

'Maybe.'

'And love exists,' I tell her, 'and unicorns run rampant

down the main streets of Burnie.'

The song changes to one about tears and songbirds.

*And wild birds sometimes fly home* is the end of my sentence and the thing I do not say.

# CHAPTER SEVEN

Auntie Kath brings me a cup of tea. Milky, two sugars. I take it with a 'thanks' and a smile. She doesn't have to bring me tea—she knows that—but she likes to do it.

'Let me look after you, sometimes,' she says. 'I know you don't need it—big, independent girl that you are. But just indulge me, once in a while, okay?'

Auntie Kath and I love English Breakfast the best. We like Darjeeling and Russian Caravan. We both hate Earl Grey. It tastes like soap.

'I wish I could be like Grandma T and bake you scones and things to nourish you. But I'm afraid tea is the best you're going to get from me.'

'Grandma T raised you to only cook if you want to,' I remind her. 'She says that being a feminist is about *choosing* whether you want to be in the kitchen.'

'I might want to be in the kitchen more, if I didn't nearly burn it down every time I turn the stove on.' Auntie Kath laughs. 'Lucky I make good art, eh?'

'You make great art. But you're getting there'—I try for encouraging—'with your baking. You're getting good.'

'Tiger, last night I made a sponge cake that looked like a

beret,' she reminds me. 'But I will get there. Even if I make a fool of myself while I'm learning.'

'Gloria Steinem said, "Whatever you want to do, just do it. Making a damn fool of yourself is absolutely essential."'

'I wonder if she said that when she was learning to make sponge cake …'

I'm warming to my theme. 'And there's this poem that Wally showed me, one day, called *Translations*. There's something about women and love and baked bread.'

'Wally, eh?' Auntie Kath interrupts. 'He's a real Renaissance man, that one.'

I shrug, my cheeks warming. 'If they had Aussie Rules during the Renaissance.'

Auntie Kath cocks an eyebrow. She is in her sculpting clothes—a ratty old t-shirt stained with clay and paint, with a pair of high-waisted jeans (circa 1995). It's her uniform. Sometimes, she sleeps in her painting clothes. She only wears a different outfit when she's got an exhibition opening for her work, or when she's coming to my school to see me perform.

I change the subject. 'The stain on your top looks like a heart.'

'That's fitting.' She smiles. 'When I dress in my art clothes, I feel like I'm being the truest representation of myself. I feel like my inside world matches my outside one. My heart is really on my sleeve.'

'Corny,' I say. But I like it, really.

I look down at my own clothes, wondering what they say about my inside world.

I'm still in my black polyester trousers and Woolies work shirt. It's crumpled now, and there's an orange stain down the front from a Fanta bottle that exploded.

The father said his toddler didn't shake it. I have my doubts. She had a bloody wicked look on her little face.

'Will Preen get this off, do you think?' I ask Auntie Kath. She reaches across me to a pot of paintbrushes, extracts a red one, and proceeds to draw a huge, wonky heart all the way across my front. 'No,' she says. 'But now your heart is on your sleeve, too.'

I sigh. 'New work shirt time.'

'I already bought you a couple in the Target sale. You can wear that one to school. You might start a trend.'

'Auntie Kath, I am the least likely person, in the whole history of people, to start a trend.' I stifle a yawn.

'Big night?'

I shake my head. 'Nah, it was okay.'

Actually, bizarrely, it had been fun. Or, as close to fun as you can ever have while wearing a pastel green shirt and a neckerchief.

Rhino, Flo and I spent our shift writing each other notes on stubs of receipt roll. Rhino sent me crazy jokes. Flo sent me cartoon sketches of Jamie being eaten by a mutant salamander. There was also the incident of a lubricant bottle tipping over behind the service desk. We discovered that no matter how well we wiped it up, the patch of floor remained slippery. And it was fun to slide on.

Jamienator told us not to: '*It's an O, H and S risk, guys!*'

'Oh, just let us crazy kids have some fun, James,' Flo said, in reply, waving him away.

His ears went bright red, and he said he was off to tell Mr Blakely, the manager. We knew that he wouldn't, really. He'd just hide behind the toilet rolls, for a while, thinking we were shaking in our boots, when really it was the best part of our night—knowing he was behind the toilet rolls with red ears.

Melody doesn't understand how I can handle working at Woolworths.

'Those neck scarves,' she cries. 'And the way people treat you! I mean, God forbid their All-Bran scans at the wrong price. I mean, I am all for honouring the work traditionally done by women, but, ugh, Resey, you are *not empowered* to stand up for yourself when people are epic douchebags to you! Doesn't that make you anxious and frustrated?'

No. Because I have Flo and Rhino, and Jamie is amusing, and there's new, weird fruit and veg to learn, and—mostly—people are friendly to you, if you're friendly to them. I like Woolworths. I like working.

'It's fun working with Rhino and Flo. But I'm buggered now,' I tell Auntie Kath.

My phone buzzes. I pull it from my pocket.

It's sooooo slllllipppperrryyyy!
How's the shirt?

'Melody?' asks Auntie Kath.

I shake my head. 'Rhino. From work. Asking me about my shirt. Also, there was an … incident. With some lubricant.'

Auntie Kath cocks an eyebrow. 'Do I want to know?'

I wrinkle my nose. 'Nothing like *that*, Auntie Kath—erk, *it's Rhino*! We just spilled it, accidentally, and then there was some sliding …'

Auntie Kath ruffles my hair. 'I'm glad that you have fun at work. I do worry about you, with all your commitments, on top of school ...'

I shrug. 'I like being busy. Which reminds me ...' I take a slurp of tea, and feel my chest warming. 'I have a monologue to learn before I go to bed. Dangerous Liaisons. *Les Liaisons Dangereuses*, in fact.'

I adopt the French accent I've been learning. *"'I learned how to look cheerful while under the table I stuck a fork into the back of my hand.'"*

'Heavy,' says Auntie Kath, eyebrows raised. 'All right then, my sweet workaholic. Go and waste your teenage years on study. But then, get some sleep.'

'It's not wasteful.' I finish my tea and take Auntie Kath's cup, too, to rinse in the sink. 'It's elucidating.'

She shakes her head. 'You're a little mystery, Therese Laurel Geeves. One minute you're talking Aussie Rules, like you swallowed Jason Dunstall; the next you're all high-brow. *Elucidating*? My giddy aunt.'

I laugh. '*Jason Dunstall*? You can tell you haven't watched football since the eighties. Anyway, who says I can't be both? Who says I can't love footy and *know how to talk good*?'

'Nobody.' Auntie Kath looks serious now. 'Tiger, nobody says you can't. Gloria Steinem definitely wouldn't say it, and neither would Grandma T.'

'Melody does. And she's the uber-feminist.'

Auntie Kath groans. 'Melody is ... still working it out,' she says. 'As are you. I'm giving Mel a free pass, because she ... God love her, she tries hard. But, if anyone else ever tells you that—'

'I'll either devastate them with my sparkling wit and extensive vocabulary, or I'll kick 'em in the nuts,' I say, as I open the lounge room door. 'Don't worry, Auntie K. I got it sorted.'

I do.

I will.

I might.

I hear Auntie Kath get up from her stool and move back over to the sculpture she's working on. It's a girl, lying on her side, sleeping; a small creature, like a baby monster, curled inside her arms. When I ask Auntie Kath what it's about, she only shrugs and says, 'Sometimes I dream that I'm the only one who can soothe the monsters to sleep.'

Dear Dad,
If I thought,
I could ever get this shit together,
I'd stick the soles of my feet to this earth
And wrap myself in its sky
To stay here forever.

# CHAPTER EIGHT

Wally isn't at training.

'Do you know where he is?' I ask Peter. He looks bemused, which gives me my answer.

I shake my head. 'He never misses training, and now two nights in a row?'

'*Two* nights?'

I forgot I haven't told Peter about yesterday and Wally and the fountain. When I do, he raises an eyebrow. 'Dodgy.'

Some girls from Grade Nine walk past, their school skirts rolled up and their top shirt buttons undone. Peter's eyes are full of pink love-hearts, like a character in a Looney Tunes cartoon.

'Focus, Pete.' I click my fingers in front of his face. 'If Melody was here, she'd—'

Peter shudders. 'I know,' he says, wearily. 'And, hey, Resey, you know I'm not a complete arsehole, like she thinks I am, don't you? I mean, sometimes I look at … at *legs*, and stuff. But I try not to. And the rest is all for show. The footy guys—'

'*Are* actual arseholes. But, trust me, Pete, we all know you're not. And, you know, Auntie Kath always says that a healthy sexual appetite is nothing to be ashamed of. But maybe you could be a bit subtler about it? Now, can we please get back to more important matters? Wally. Not at training.'

The Grade Nine girls finally look our way and one of them curls their lip when they see Peter staring. My heart hurts a bit for him then. Despite all the bravado, Peter's not the sort of boy those girls go for. He's not the sort of boy they're here for.

Peter is weedy and nerdy and, even though he loves footy, he's not great at it. That never stops him trying out though. Every year he pulls on his footy shorts and boots, and trots out there. Every year he trots back and says, 'Always next season, Resey. Always next season.'

Those girls don't want a boy like Peter. And when he tries to make up for it, by being extra macho, it only ends up making it worse. Those girls want the boys with bulging biceps and permanent spots as full-forward or ruck. They want a trophy boyfriend.

They want Nick Wallace.

But Wally's not here.

'I'm going to find him,' I say, pushing myself up from the bench.

'Using what?' Peter follows me away from the field, towards the bus stop.

'He was at the fountain yesterday. Maybe he's there again today.'

'What's the big deal?' Peter's caught up to me now. 'So he misses training a couple of times. Maybe he's not feeling well.'

'He didn't hang out with us at lunch time, either,' I

point out. 'Was he in class?' Peter and Wally are in the same core classes. The only electives I share with him are art and English lit, and we don't have those on Wednesdays.

'Yeah, he was in class,' Peter says. 'Wally's always in class. He never wags.'

'He never usually wags footy,' I remind him.

Peter nods. 'Good call, Resey. So, the fountain you reckon? Hey, don't you have musical stuff on now?'

I shake my head. 'Cancelled. Mr Lohrey's in Hobart, I think, for some teacher professional development thing. I'm free to go on a Wally Hunt.'

'*Where's Wally?*' Peter says, quietly. He sticks out his hand, as the Metro bus approaches.

I don't really believe he'll be there. It seems too simple. In a movie, this would be the beginning of an epic quest— possibly with clues and coded messages—sending me and Peter all around Burnie, seeking our best mate. Jointley's, the big creepy octopus sculpture, the West Park Oval grandstands, Fern Glade, or the Roundhill lookout. Peter and I would race around town, picking up breadcrumbs; learning about Wally; learning about ourselves. There might be a montage to the backing track of a song by Ed Sheeran.

In the end, we'd find him *and* ourselves, and everything would make sense.

Everything would wrap up in a neat bow.

In real life there are almost never neat bows.

In real life everything is messy.

In real life we find Wally by the fountain.

'Oi! Wallace!' Peter's voice echoes around the plaza. I jab him in the ribs. I'd been hoping for a subtler entrance.

'Sorry,' Peter says. 'You go first.'

Wally turns to look at us. His face splits into a huge, slanting grin. He doesn't look fussed about being caught out. 'Champ! Johnson! G'day!'

'Hi, Wally,' I say, as Pete thumps down next to Wally. I hover awkwardly opposite them. There's nowhere else to sit. Wally looks over at me. He stands up.

'Park here, Champ.'

And I want to. I want to sit and gaze up at him and feel his warmth; the sunshine that radiates off him because he is golden.

But I shake my head. Can't have him thinking I'm some feeble female he has to leave his seat for. 'I'm 'right, Wally. You stay there.'

'We should all go somewhere else,' Wally says. 'You fellas up for chips? I can hear Jointley's calling my name.'

'You're meant to be at training,' Pete says, jabbing at Wally's arm as we walk into the sunlight.

'Who are you, my mother?'

Peter laughs. 'Hannah would be ecstatic to know you're not at training.'

'True.' Wally rolls his eyes. 'She'd have me wrapped in cotton wool and kept in the cupboard if she could find a ball of wool big enough. *I'm all she has left*!' he says, in a melodramatic voice.

'So, why weren't you at training?' Peter persists. I'm seriously regretting bringing him along. I thought he'd be cool but, of course, I should have known. It's about footy. Pete is incapable of being cool about footy.

Wally points to his knee. 'Did it on the weekend, coming

down from the bounce at the start of the last quarter. Don't want Holland to notice it. He'll have a fit, and there's no way he'll let me play against Clarence. I just need to give it a couple of days and it'll be right as rain. I have to play against the Roos. Holland reckons there will be an AFL scout there because they've got MacMichael playing and, well, Holland reckons we're the ones the scouts will be looking out for. So I have to play. This could be my big shot. I can't risk Holland seeing me hobbling around. He'll bench me.'

I'm relieved. Relieved that it's just a knee and nothing more. I just hope it's fine by Saturday. Because, what if he isn't at the top of his game then? What if the scout does come and Wally munts a bounce, or drops a mark, or kicks the ball to the opposition?

What if he loses his dream all because of a stupid knee?

What if—?

'Resey, don't look so stressed!' Wally punches me on the arm. 'Seriously, the knee will be fine. It's nearly back to normal now. I'll be awesome by the weekend.'

'I was worried,' I say, ignoring the way my arm feels hot now—not from pain but because Wally touched it. 'You missed training two days and you were just staring at the fountain ...'

'Making a wish,' Wally says, shrugging. 'Throwing in a five-cent piece and ... you know. Any bit of luck I can get, I'll take it. I'll be wearing my lucky guernsey too. And my dad's lucky socks.'

'That's just gross,' Peter says, wrinkling his nose. 'Those things are festy.'

'Shut up, Pete,' Wally growls, but he's smiling.

We get to Jointley's.

'I'll shout your chips,' I say. 'For more luck.'

'You don't have to do that, Champ.'

'I want to. Chiko roll as well.'

'Okay, but I'm shouting after the game on Saturday,' Wally says. 'I'll buy spiders too. We'll celebrate, all right? It'll be great.'

I nod. 'Sure thing, Wally.'

And I hope. I hope enormously we do have something to celebrate. I hope the scout loves Wally. I hope his dreams come true.

But, at the same time, there's a gnawing inside of me. Because if the scout does pick Wally, then he's gone. And when he goes, the light goes, too.

Wally winks at me then and passes me a piece of folded paper. I open it, while he and Peter are at the counter.

There's a smiley face drawn on the paper and underneath, it says:

*Don't worry 'bout a thing, because every little thing gonna be all right.*

I can't help the smile that spreads across my face. He quotes poetry, but he also quotes Bob Marley. He's everything. He's everything, to me.

Dear Dad,
One day,
I want you to see me flying.

# CHAPTER NINE

Wally and I are sitting in the chook shed surrounded by a gang of rowdy pullets. We've raised them since they were chicks—Hodge, Mitchell, Franklin and Rioli. Wally named them after his favourite AFL players. I pointed out that 'Franklin' isn't a very girly name for a hen, but he said that's okay. Who says Franklin's a girl, just because there's no comb on its fuzzy head?

'Maybe they're non-binary,' he said that day, when he gave them their names. 'Maybe it's not up to us to ascribe a gender to them, just because of their anatomy.'

'Then … maybe it's wrong to name them at all,' I pointed out. 'Maybe we should just let them choose their own identities.'

'Fair call,' he said, 'but I like naming things. How about we give them footy player names for now and when they're older they can tell us if the names match how they feel inside.'

'They'll tell us in chook language?'

'They'll communicate it, somehow,' he insisted.

'If you could have any name, what would it be?' I asked him.

He thought for a moment. Then, he smiled. 'Robert.

Lots of good poets called Robert. Robert Frost, Robert Browning, Robert Graves ... also, Robert DiPierdomenico, Hawthorn legend.'

I rolled my eyes. 'Always comes back to the footy.'

'What about you?' he asked.

I just shrugged. 'I don't know. I guess I'd keep the names I have. I have a few, already. More than enough.'

'But if you could have just *one* name?'

Then and there, I couldn't honestly think of anything. Wally answered so quickly; with such certainty. I wasn't certain about anything. Not even my own name. Not even my choice for a name. Not even my *self*.

'I dunno,' I'd said. 'I'll go with Franklin. In case Franklin rejects the name.'

Franklin hasn't rejected the name yet. At least, not that we know. She's gone on to assert her femininity by being the most prolific layer in the shed. She kicks up a stink every time Rioli tries to come near her; makes it perfectly clear that any egg-fertilising is going to be done on her terms. And definitely not until she's finished eating.

Then, she makes him work for it; makes him court her; makes him value her.

And he does. Rioli loves Franklin the best of all the chooks.

As if energised by his love, she gives eggs aplenty; big, golden-yolked and delicious.

Wally and I have already collected all the eggs, today. We're sitting in the hay, watching our grown-up babies prance and flirt and eat and gossip. Wally is turning an egg round and around in his hand, like it's a precious stone.

'Thanks for coming over this arvo,' I say. 'Grandma T appreciates it.'

Grandma T asked Wally over, to help her with 'something on her computer'. We both knew it was just a pretence. Grandma T is a scientist. Back in the seventies, she used to *build* computers.

She just wants to check that Wally is okay.

I told her about the big game tomorrow and Wally's knee and the fountain and everything. She had to make sure he is happy. *And* stuffed full of ginger cake.

He ate three pieces. He's fine.

'I like your grandma so much,' Wally says, licking his fingers. And then, slowly, he brushes a hair off my face. The skin on my cheek zings. 'I like you. You know that, don't you, Resey?'

'Of course I know that,' I say, quickly. 'We're best friends.'

I say it because I'm scared if I don't say it, he might.

And then I say, 'We should get in. Grandma T has more food for you. She's going to heal your knee with butter and golden syrup.'

I wait.

I wait for him to say, 'No, I want to stay. I want to stay here with you, alone. I want to sit with you, here, and pick apart all the mysteries of the universe. You're the only one I want to be with. The only one I can talk to, like *that*.'

But he doesn't, of course. Instead, I get, 'Great, I'm starving.' And then, as we walk back towards the house with our baskets of eggs, he says, 'You've still got chook poo on your face. I thought I got it, but I didn't.'

The wind drops. I'm with it.

# CHAPTER TEN

I look at myself in the bathroom mirror full of sighs.

It's Saturday morning. Big game day. I still look the same.

I make a checklist of pieces of me. Scattered, incongruent, missing the glue that should make them match—that should make me into a person.

Limp, faded-brown hair.

Freckled nose, bent and swerving sideways.

Lips like a knife edge.

Goggly, staring eyes like that slow loris in the meme.

And below the eyes, below the face, a body made by Picasso.

Skinny chook legs, wide hips, boobs that still struggle to fill a crop top made for tweens. Boobs that made Emma Houston look at me with that smug little smile. The one that says, *You're faulty.*

Emma Houston has boobs like a painting by Rubens. Emma is shaped like a figure-eight. Emma has wavy, strawberry-blonde hair like a Pantene ad and pillowy lips like Scarlett Johansson. And her nose is straight. I saw the photos from last year's best-and-fairest: she looked like a goddess. She had a spray tan. *A spray tan.* Like a freaking Instagram model.

She looked like the sort of girl the players take to the

Brownlow. She's glossy and perfect. Nobody takes girls like me to the Brownlow. I'm the girl who had chook poo on her face last night. I'm the girl who makes him scones.

Usually, I don't care much how I look, but on footy days …

I want to look different today; better. I want Wally to spot me in the crowd, after he wins the bounce that makes the scout sit up. Wally will see me there … and *see me*.

Maybe want to take me with him when he goes to uni.

Would I go?

I think of everything I have here in the little town I love— Auntie Kath and this house and all the memories. Grandma T, Melody and Roz, Rhino and Flo. The musical and the school band. Writing, art, Woolies.

I like it here. I like my life. But if Wally was gone, there'd be moth-holes in everything.

Would I go with him if he asked me?

He won't ask me.

Bent nose, freckly face, flat chest. He won't ask me. Even though he and Emma have broken up, I'll never stand a chance. Because there are other girls like Emma, and Wally will be with one of them. Even though the world seems screwy in many ways, there are some things that are certain.

I look at the picture I have of my mum hanging on the wall. I can see bits of me in her. The thin lips and freckles.

*The eyes.*

But while on me they look too round, too alien—on her they sparkle.

She was someone a boy would pick out in the crowd.

I tug on my team guernsey. At least it hides the non-existent chest and the way my waist goes out when it should go in.

I'm wearing my skinny jeans with it—the black ones, with the rips that Roz says are fashionable. I wish I looked as good in jeans as Melody does, or that I had the guts to wear some fancy sandals, or a pin-up dress like Roz does, or even high heels instead of my usual Dunlop Volleys.

The other girls wear their guernseys tight, and they wear strappy stilettos or glittery thongs; they wear makeup. When Roz wears makeup, she looks polished and fancy. When I wear makeup, I just look pretend.

This is me.

I'm stuck with it.

I'll always be the girl with the chook poo on her face. Wally might tell me his dreams; he might tell me poetry; he might talk to me about clouds and the sea and God and the extent of the universe—the things he never talks about to anyone else—but sometimes I feel as if he's talking to a wall. As if I'm just something blank and silent that he can throw his strange wonderings at; see what pictures they make on my pale surface.

'Are you digging a hole to China in there?' Auntie Kath calls over the top of the Pretenders CD she's painting to. 'I thought you wanted to be at the game at eleven?'

I look at my watch. *Bugger*. 'Coming!' I cry. I take a tube of lip gloss from the top bathroom drawer (a gift from Roz aeons ago) and I glob a bit on.

No difference. Still me, only with shiny lips now.

'You look nice,' says Auntie Kath when I emerge from the bathroom. I know she's only saying it because I took so long in there. She must know I've been *trying*.

She wipes her paint-splattered hands on my old work

shirt and passes me a Tupperware container full of energy slices. I baked them last night. On footy days I don't cook for only Wally. I always try and bring the team something home-made. Something that isn't oranges or Powerade. 'Come on, Tiger,' Auntie Kath says. 'Let's go and watch these boys of yours. Are we picking up Melody and Roz?'

I nod. 'Yep. If that's okay.'

'It's always been okay and always will be.' Auntie Kath smiles.

'You have paint on your cheek,' I tell her.

'Do I look like Siouxsie?' she asks.

'You look nothing like Siouxsie,' I tell her.

'Dammit,' she curses. She grabs a flannel and wipes her face. She grins, cheekily, and turns up the song that's playing on the CD player. I know this one, too. Whenever Auntie Kath needs a boost, she puts it on. I've never really understood why it's called 'Brass in Pocket', but I can't help admitting that the joy of it is kind of infectious. Auntie Kath shimmies her shoulders and pouts.

'Yes, Auntie Kath,' I say, rolling my eyes. 'I get it. You are completely *special*.'

Roz is at Melody's place. They're eating noodles on the deck. 'Mum made you some, too.' Melody hands me a paper box, as she gets in the car. It smells of soy and lemongrass.

I look up at the Kwong's lounge room window. Lexi is standing there, watching, dressed in a band tee and black leather pants. She waves. I grin and wave back. She moves towards the stereo and a recent Aussie hip-hop hit—all casual swearing and cheeky drug references—break-dances out the front door. I see Lexi, inside, shaking her hips and rapping along.

'Your mum's amazing,' I say.

Melody nods. 'She is. I am trying to school her on cultural appropriation, though. She won't be told. She thinks Tkay Maidza is her homegirl.'

'Who's Tkay Maidza?' asks Roz. She looks bashful. 'Sorry, my parents hate hip hop. It's twenty-four-seven Classic FM at our place.'

'My mum would take great pleasure in commencing your education,' Melody says. 'I'll get her to make you a Spotify playlist. Plug in your headphones and the Count and Countess of Grantham will be none the wiser.'

I open the box Melody brought me and inhale the noodles. I hadn't noticed I was so hungry.

Then, swallowing, I realise there is garlic in there too, with the soy and lemongrass. 'Please tell me one of you has Tic Tacs,' I say.

'Chewie,' Melody replies, offering a battered packet from her jeans pocket. 'Can't have you breathing on Nick Wallace with garlic breath.'

'And why would she be breathing on Nick Wallace?' Auntie Kath sounds amused.

'I won't be,' I reply, quickly. 'Let's just get there, okay?'

I look out the window at the ocean and the blue, blue sky. All the pieces of me are breaking apart; floating away. I am a shapeless, formless thing, waiting for someone to tell me what to be.

Maybe waiting for Wally to tell me.

Waiting for him to see that we're the same. Waiting for him to see me. For him to catch me. For us to give each other a soft place to land.

Dear Dad,
Today I will fly.
Watch out for me below.
Today I might soar high enough
To just feel you again.

# CHAPTER ELEVEN

Wally's dad died in a building site fall. He was an engineer. It was raining. They told him not to go up so high. But it rains six days out of seven here in winter, and they were already behind time.

It only took a moment and a look to the left when it should have been right; a foot in the wrong place.

So Hannah lost a husband. Wally lost a dad.

Just an hour before, Hannah had made breakfast for her husband, Mike—peanut butter on toast and a tub of low-fat yoghurt. Mike was on a new health kick. The doctor had told him that he had high blood pressure. He'd decided just that morning to start running every day and to eat fewer bags of Jointley's chips.

He had a growing son. He had to start looking after himself. He needed to be healthy for the boy.

But then it rained six days out of seven.

It was a tragedy—a huge one, in this small town. I may not have known Wally when he arrived in my Grade Seven classroom, but *everyone* knew who Mike Wallace was.

It was *terribly, terribly sad*.

He was a footballer. Like his son, he was a ruckman—

height runs in the family. He won the best-and-fairest medal, for the Hawks four years running. He only retired when Wally was born. His face is in photos on the clubroom walls, just like his son's.

When I met Nick Wallace, that first day in Grade Seven, I didn't know he was Mike Wallace's son. I didn't know he'd lost his dad the same year I lost mine.

We had both been three years old.

One night, when we were down by the beach behind the Makers Workshop, eating Dave's Noodles from cardboard boxes, I asked him what his parents did for jobs.

'Mum's a nurse,' he said, picking a hard bit of fried onion from the top of his mie goreng. 'She works at Doctor Jensen's practice in town. My dad's dead. Ages ago. I was only a little kid. I don't remember him at all.'

'Oh, bugger, Wally,' I said, putting down my plastic fork.

He lifted a shoulder. He was going for *indifferent*, but his face was tense. It still hurt him inside. I could tell.

'He was kind of a superstar,' Wally sighed. 'Captain of the football team, went to uni, got a great job, had this beautiful wife and new little kid. Everyone in town knew his name. Everyone loved Mike Wallace. Everyone remembers him.'

'Wait, your dad was Mike Wallace?'

Wally gave me a small smile. 'See? *Everyone*.'

'He was a legend,' I said, putting my hand lightly on Wally's arm, wishing my fingers didn't tremble so much. Wishing I didn't feel my stomach fall to the ground every time my skin touched his.

'And that's the way everyone remembers him,' Wally

said. 'So it's not all bad. Dying young, when everyone still thinks you're a hero, before you get old and grey and bent. There's advantages to that.' He stared for a moment out at the sea. 'It's why I like poetry,' he said, after a while. 'Because he did, too. He took a unit in it at uni. But he only ever read it in secret because, you know, "footy players don't read poetry; they don't have feelings". He never told anyone about it, except Mum. She kept all of his books. I read all of them, soon as I learned to read. I liked them better than my picture books. Anyway ...' He shook his head, curls bouncing. He poked at his now-cold dinner. 'I'm so over these noodles. Let's go to Jointley's. Healthy food sucks.'

So we went to Jointley's and ordered egg-and-beetroot burgers. We stopped talking about sad stuff and I didn't tell him then about *my* father.

When we walked home along the beach, our chins sticky with sauce and beetroot juice, Wally slowed, took my hand again and pointed at a seagull pestering some small kids for a chip.

'I'd like to be him,' he said.

'A seagull?'

'*That* seagull,' he said. 'All it knows is food and sleep and warmth and the wide blue sky. I'd like that.'

'No worries, you mean?' I asked. 'Besides where your next chip is coming from?'

'Wouldn't it be sweet?' Wally said. 'Just chips and the sun and all the empty nothingness.'

'Do you know any poems about seagulls?' I asked him.

Wally shook his head; shot me a shy grin. 'Maybe I'll write one,' he said.

Dear Dad,

I read somewhere that your soul has a weight;

That when you die your body lessens.

When you went my body got heavier.

I am too heavy now.

I want to be a soul;

Seagull light.

# CHAPTER TWELVE

As soon as I see him, I know the knee isn't better.

It's not that he's hobbling or limping or favouring his right leg over his left one. It's just … he's running *different*. Wally doesn't run like that. Wally runs like he has springs in his legs, like there's joy in every stride. Today Wally runs like he's made of stones.

He's not smiling.

Wally always smiles when he's coming onto a footy ground.

I wave to him as he passes. He doesn't wave back.

He doesn't see me. He's *inside*. And I know that what's in there is dark today. Wally knows that his knee isn't better. He knows that the AFL scout is here. Holland spotted him, and told the boys, and Faulsy told Peter, when they were lined up for pies. And Peter told everyone.

The scout's the bloke in the black hat. He has a little notepad, and a look on his face like he's important. There's a girl next to him, in a navy suit, who's already brought him three coffees and a Chiko Roll. He didn't eat the Chiko Roll. He only sniffed it and gave it back to the girl. She ate it, looking like she was going to cry.

That guy's the scout for sure, and Wally's knee's not better.

For the first half things go well. A new guy is up against Wally instead of MacMichael. I've never seen him before— must be from the reserves. He's terrible. Wally wins every single bounce and there's a flicker of joy on his face, dancing on top of the determination. There's still a tiny wince whenever he hits the ground.

At half time, the boys are four goals up. I give Wally a muesli slice and he says, 'Thanks, Champ. You see me out there? Do I look okay?'

'Wally, you look amazing!' He is looking good out there, despite everything.

'Thanks, you,' he says, and his fingers brush my cheek.

'Chook poo?' I ask, my own fingers searching for wetness on my skin. I didn't feed the chooks, this morning, and I checked the mirror fifty times, before I left. 'Sauce?' I sigh, thinking of the noodles.

'No,' he says. 'Just you. Just … thanks for saying I'm doing well. When you say that it makes me believe it.'

Peter's at my side, his scarf wrapped twice around his neck, against the August chill. I'm not even feeling it.

'You're doing awesome, mate,' he says, and for once there isn't that hint of envy—that undercurrent of, *Man, I wish I was out there.* Peter is happy for Wally. We all are. Melody even brings him a Powerade. This is a big deal. Usually Melody sends us to the soft drink van. She prefers the coffee stand. It's run by hipster activists.

The indie-girl at the coffee stand today has cropped bleached hair, a nose stud and a picture of Rosie the Riveter on her arm. Even though Melody doesn't believe in love, she does believe in hipster girls with retro feminist tattoos.

'My parents would call that girl a wastrel,' Roz says. She bites her lip and adds, 'But I really like her tattoo.'

'I really like everything about her,' Melody breathes. 'How many coffees do you think I can order before it starts looking sus?'

The soft drink stand is manned by a very non-hipster bloke called Nige, who might have been behind that counter since 1879. The fact that Melody bought Wally his Powerade, instead of getting herself another cappuccino, says it all. She wants Wally to do well, as much as the rest of us do.

As much as *I* do.

Because even though there's still that tiny part of me that aches at the thought of him leaving, my hope for him is much bigger.

I can still feel his fingers on my cheek. They felt like he might say, *Come with me.*

'How's your knee?' I whisper to him, trying to ignore his scent as my mouth is at his ear.

Peppermint.

Sweat.

Lynx deodorant.

Wally.

He shrugs. 'It's far from perfect, Champ. It's bloody sore. But I'm doing okay despite it, don't you think? Lucky that Clarence newbie isn't giving me much competition. Dunno where MacMichael is today but I'm not complaining!'

'You're doing fantastically,' I say. 'You can't tell at all about the knee.'

Wally grins. 'Thanks, Resey. And thanks for, you know, being here.'

The siren sounds for the start of the second half. Wally inhales the rest of his slice. 'Nice chef work, you!' he says.

If I was Wally's manager, on the mainland, I'd make him slices every weekend. And banana muffins.

'Well, wish me luck!' He hip-and-shoulders me and I fake that it hurts. I can't wipe the grin from my face, though. I'm so excited for him.

He runs back to the ground like he has springs in his legs.

But, as he reaches the centre circle, the springs rust. The rubbish ruckman from Clarence is back on the interchange bench. Standing in the centre of the field, stretching his hamstring, is Tom MacMichael—Clarence's star ruckman and best-and-fairest for the club two years running.

It all makes sense. The Clarence coach was resting Macca in the first half to give him the best chance of playing well in the second. The best chance of helping the Roos win and the best chance of impressing the scout.

And, as he bounces from foot to foot, it looks like he swallowed the Energiser bunny.

Wally glances our way. He's terrified.

'Go, Wally!' I yell, as Peter roars, 'Carn the Hawks!'

'Go, Hawkies!' Roz screams.

Melody rolls her eyes and mutters, 'Down with the patriarchy.'

I cross my fingers and, inside my Volleys, I cross my toes, but my belly's already sinking. Wally doesn't look good out there. His confidence is shattered, and everyone knows that confidence is almost as important as form in a game of footy.

It's a psychological war on that ground, and Wally's already on the back foot.

And then it begins. The umpire bounces the ball. It ricochets off the muddy soil and right in Wally's direction. It should be an easy one for him. But he doesn't leap high enough. He doesn't leap far enough.

MacMichael gets it.

He gets it, and his tap sees the ball heading straight in the direction of Carpenter, one of Clarence's best forwards. Carpenter takes the mark and heads towards the attacking fifty for Clarence. He easily dodges Pedda and punts the ball at Wise, the Clarence full-forward.

Wise collects the mark and takes his time, lining up.

The ball goes through the middle posts, like a hot knife through butter.

Wally's dead scared now.

He's starting to limp, too.

The scout is taking notes.

My muesli slice is useless. So's the Powerade. Nothing's going to work if Wally's scared. We're screwed. And I feel like I'm going to vomit up my pie and Coke.

# CHAPTER THIRTEEN

I fix all my hope and all my will and all the luck that the universe might have been planning to give *me* on Nick Wallace. Any magic I might have inside me—that goes to him too.

I've splashed my drink all down my front—it's wet and uncomfortable. My hair is a mess in the wind, my lips are chapped and my eyes are streaming, but it doesn't matter.

None of that shit—all the things I thought when I looked in the mirror—matter anymore.

Everything is Wally.

Roz squeezes my arm. 'He'll be okay, Resey. It'll all be okay.'

I don't reply; can't reply. What can I say?

Everything is Wally.

He's limping and he's broken and it's hopeless, but I'm still willing him on.

I stare at him. My eyes are a camera lens. He's in the middle of everything. He's the centre of everything.

'Come on, Wally,' I murmur.

'This is shit,' Peter says. 'He's stuffed.'

'Can we go to Jointley's already?' groans Melody. 'This is painful.'

'Mel,' Roz says, gently. I see her shake her head.

I don't see Melody roll her eyes, but I can almost feel it.

I don't care. I don't care what she does; what she thinks. My whole soul is with him.

I don't blink.

Wally looks away from the ball for just a moment. He sees me watching.

He nods.

The whistle blows.

When the final siren sounds the Hawks fans yelp and holler.

The team surrounds Wally. They scream and yell and hug him and kiss him, forgetting for a moment that they like to be tough and unemotional and *blokes*.

I watch the scout approach Holland.

And I think, *That's it. I've lost him.*

Because that last goal was magic. And the scout saw it.

I'm crying. I don't know why I'm crying.

Wally looks at me again. I expect him to smile, but he only looks.

And I can't read his expression. I can't read *him*. Why isn't he smiling?

I don't know whether to go to the car park and wait for him. Usually, I do. To offer congratulations, or a home-baked something, and a sympathetic smile. It's tradition. Wally expects it.

But today feels ... different. I don't know if he'll expect me. I don't know if he'll want me there.

Why isn't he smiling?

Peter can see the indecision on my face. He shakes his

head. 'Better leave him, Resey,' he says, softly. 'Reckon he'll be pretty busy with Holland after this. Bloody legend.'

'He might come to Jointley's,' I say, hopefully. 'When he's all done?'

Peter doesn't look convinced, but he knows I need to hold on to that hope, cotton-thin as it is. 'Yeah, maybe. You wanna go?'

I nod, looking to Melody and Roz.

'Yeah, of course,' says Roz. 'There's a pasty there with my name on it. I've only got homework waiting for me at home, and my mum going mad at me for spending the day at the footy—it's so "uncouth" and such a "waste of my time and talents".' Roz rolls her eyes like she doesn't care, but I know she does. Her parents are a nightmare. 'I'm staying at Jointley's for as long as humanly possible.'

'He probably won't show,' Melody says, linking her arm through mine. 'I'm thinking the boys will be taking him for a sneaky beer or two at Greens, don't you? But that's okay. We can all have a good chat.'

My head still jerks up whenever the plastic curtain rustles at the front of Jointley's. The others natter happily about school, Netflix shows and Wally's future stardom.

I'm just waiting for him to come.

'I think it's time to go, Resey.' Melody is abnormally gentle, when she forces me to give up, after more than an hour of watching the door.

In the car, on the way home, the radio is playing a nineties Spice Girls' song. Rhino would love it. Auntie Kath starts singing along.

Melody joins in—she and I both learned the song by

osmosis when we were babies. Roz, of course, was raised on Bach and Beethoven, so she only hums.

I stay silent. I lean my elbow on the car window and watch as the rain begins to drizzle from the eggshell-grey sky.

'You okay, Tiger?' Auntie Kath asks. 'Was the game okay?'

'The scout was there,' I say. 'And Wally was a hero.'

'Well, that's good ... isn't it?'

'It's wonderful.'

It is.

It *is* wonderful.

We stop at the Kwongs' house and I tell Melody and Roz that I'll see them at school, even though we had sort-of plans to go to the park tomorrow.

'What about—' Melody begins. Roz elbows her in the ribs. I smile at her, gratefully.

'Come on,' she tells Melody. 'I'll come in for a while. I'll tell Mum I had to borrow some of your biology notes.'

'I'm not taking—' Melody begins to protest.

Roz shakes her head, her eyes wide and fierce.

Melody shuts up.

'Bye, Resey!' they call out, waving as Mabel backs smoothly out of the driveway.

'Can we go to Grandma T's?' I ask Auntie Kath, as we leave Melody's street.

Auntie Kath puts on her indicator, and we turn right onto Seabrook Road, heading in the direction of the farm.

When we arrive, I give Grandma T a hug. 'I think I just need to go to the chook shed.'

'Unicorns?' Grandma T asks. She knows. The chook

shed is one of the few places where I can lose myself. I can turn everything off and imagine I'm in the Otherwhere.

'Unicorns,' I reply.

In the shed, I sit in the dark. I don't eat my cake. I feel like I'm not breathing, but I must be, because I can hear myself crying.

When he comes, it feels like a dream at first. I'd wanted him there so strongly. But then he talks. 'Grandma T said I could come out.'

'I thought you'd be getting pissed with the boys,' I say, my voice splintering a bit.

Something is different.

Something is charged.

'They wanted to. I wanted you.'

He leans into me. He puts his head on my shoulder, at first, and I hear him say something that sounds like, 'Make it feel okay.'

And then he raises his head.

Raises his lips.

It's magic.

And I think, *Maybe he's not lost. Maybe he'll take me with him. This has to mean he'll take me with him.*

He strokes my face. 'Golden,' he whispers.

He doesn't quote poetry; doesn't say another word.

He looks like he might cry.

I'm filled with stardust. I'm filled with the whole world.

Dear Dad,
I wanted to fly to you.
I wanted to land somewhere safe.
I soared and in those arms I was bathed in light.
This room is so dark now.
I'm not high enough.

# CHAPTER FOURTEEN

When we get to school, Wally isn't at his locker. He isn't there at recess or lunch or in the classes we have together.

'He's probably already on the plane to Tullamarine,' Peter says. I'm holding half a Paddle Pop, watching the ice cream drizzle down my wrist. Wally loves Paddle Pops. 'En route to Glenferrie,' Peter adds, as if we all didn't know what he meant.

'He wouldn't leave without saying goodbye.' Roz looks up from her study, shaking her head. There is a biro stuck through the auburn bun on the crown of her head.

Peter shrugs. 'Never know,' he says, taking a bite from his Vegemite sandwich.

Roz looks at me and smiles, and even though I know she doesn't *know*, I feel my cheeks heat up.

I've been blushing a lot today. Every time I close my eyes, I'm in the chook shed. In the Otherwhere. In his arms.

I wrap the rest of the ice cream in its plastic and put it on the grass.

He might come.

'Hey! I'll have that!' Melody cries and lunges for the ice cream. She grabs it before I can protest and talks through yellow mush. 'Mum's got the flu, so she's in bed listening to AB

Original instead of cooking. I'm suffering from major nutrient deficiencies, which are adversely affecting my mental health. All I've got for lunch is a fruit bun. My mind needs protein.'

'I'll eat it,' says Peter. 'I love fruit buns. And my brain doesn't care about protein. I'd still be Einstein if I ate nothing but jelly beans and Spam.'

'Spam is protein, Einstein,' Melody snaps.

'I don't think you should be too confident about exactly *what* Spam is, Kwong,' Peter retorts. He lowers his voice. 'Nobody really knows.'

'Can I have your sanger, then?' asks Roz, looking longingly at the wax-paper parcel in Peter's hands. I know for a fact that Vegemite isn't allowed in Roz's house.

'Get it into ya,' says Peter, pinging it over to her.

And so the lunch-swapping game begins and everyone forgets about Wally.

*Except for me.*

Despite what Peter says, I know Wally's not already gone. He wouldn't go without saying goodbye. Not after the chook shed. He'll take me with him.

*His hand shook when he touched my face ...*

After school, I have musical practice. I stand on the stage, waiting for Jarrod to come and sing with me, then give me the kiss that makes his girlfriend, Mandy, stupid with envy. I'm on autopilot. All I can think about is Wally.

Jarrod's lips are soggy. They move up and down like a wind-up caterpillar.

*Wally's lips breathed his soul inside me and stole mine back inside him.*

I want those lips again.

'Therese?'

I look up. Mr Lohrey is watching me, baton in hand, waiting to start the song.

I nod. 'Sorry. Just getting focussed.'

Mr Lohrey smiles, approvingly. He's always telling us to take a moment to get 'centred' and 'aligned'. 'You've come up in leaps and bounds, Resey,' he says. 'You're going to steal the show.'

Usually, this would make my heart sing. Not today.

My heart is too full of him.

I force a smile. Beside me, Jarrod makes a show of concentrating, too, desperate for Mr Lohrey's approval.

Jarrod wants to be an actor when he leaves school. He wants to go to NIDA.

Sometimes, when I switch off my brain for long enough; when I stop thinking about sensible and smart; when I'm sitting on the beach with my shoes off, letting myself just *be* … I know that I want it too.

When I'm on stage, letting the words of the script flow through me like I'm the character and these things I'm saying are real … those times, I want it more than anything. Those times, I feel free of everything. Those times, I feel alive.

*Usually*. Usually, when I'm on stage, acting, I feel complete.

Today, I feel like a million scattered pieces, searching for a home. All I want is to see Wally. Everything else feels like pretending.

I turn on my Audrey smile. I put on my Audrey voice. I open my mouth and Audrey sings.

But, inside, I'm still Tiger and inside all I can think of is *him*.

Dear Dad,
I've stopped dreaming.
I want to dream again.

# CHAPTER FIFTEEN

In my head, there's only Wally.

I feel like if you opened me up the sky would be flooded with stardust.

So when Auntie Kath sits down beside me by the window and says, 'You look like you're full of things that need to be talked about with your doting auntie,' I talk through my teeth. I don't talk long. I talk very quietly and, instead of saying *his* name, I ask Auntie Kath about the one thing that will distract her.

I ask her about my dad.

'Did he ever want to play footy professionally? Could he have been scouted like ...' I don't finish the sentence. *Like Wally*. Auntie Kath knows me so well. She would know if I said his name.

Auntie Kath settles back into the cushions. She shakes her head. 'No. He never wanted to do it professionally. I think Birdie would have liked him to; she had these dreams of being a WAG—they didn't call them that in those days, of course. She would have liked to go to the Brownlow. She would have loved to meet Warwick Capper, if only so she could tell the story.'

'I can't imagine her as a footballer's wife,' I say, looking across the room at her photo on the mantelpiece. 'I can't imagine her in a glittery dress. I so can't imagine her with a spray tan and chicken fillets in her bra.'

Auntie Kath laughs. 'Well, for one thing, chicken fillets and spray tans didn't exist in the eighties. If they had, I doubt my sister would have used them, anyway. She barely ever wore makeup. I was always the one trying to fix myself— you've seen the pictures of my terrible perm.' Auntie Kath laughs and rolls her eyes. 'It took me a very long time to be comfortable in my own skin. Becoming an artist helped. I learned that there are lots of kinds of beautiful. But back then I was always desperate to change myself. To make myself beautiful. To find my soulmate.'

'Do you still want one?' I ask, a cold shard of ice settling in my chest. 'A soulmate? You don't sometimes wish—'

Auntie Kath cuts me off. 'No,' she says, firmly. 'Not now. Maybe later. For now, I'm happy just us.'

'Are you sure?' I murmur. 'I mean, if I wasn't here, then—'

Auntie Kath inclines her head to one side. 'Tiger, you're not holding me back from anything. You never have. If I want … someone, I'll find them. But for now, it's just you and me, kid. And I'm happy, as long as I've got you. You're the closest thing to a soulmate that I've ever had. All right?'

I nod. 'I want you to be happy.'

She grips my hand. 'I *am*. I was a different person when I was young. Your Grandma T is brilliant, but she was never the most … affectionate mother. Birdie never seemed to need it. She was born independent. But I was needy. I'm not anymore. You get to a certain age, and you realise … you have to be your own best friend. You have to love yourself. Even if you're in …' She gestures down at her grubby overalls. 'Even if you only ever wear fancy dresses to school concerts.'

'I still can't imagine my mum in a fancy dress,' I say, circling back to the beginning.

'She was never just one thing,' Auntie Kath says. 'She was like you. She loved music and movies. She loved school. She loved your dad. She loved football. She loved The Cure and The Bangles. She loved *The Godfather* and *The Sound of Music*. She never wore makeup, but she did wear a dress, once or twice a year, and she looked just like Elle Macpherson when she did. She was a million different things your mum. So grounded, and yet running off to unicorns and elves. She couldn't be pinned down. She was everything, Tiger. Just like you.'

Auntie Kath winks and ruffles my hair. I love her more than Nutella.

I leave her on the window seat, watching the sky. Going up to my room, I lie on my bed for a while.

I think about my mum and dad and the chook shed and the Otherwhere and how now there's a new love story set in Grandma T's garden.

I can still feel his hands shaking.

I can still feel his lips.

I have to talk to him.

'He's not here,' says Hannah when I go over. Her voice is a bit unsteady; a bit nervous. 'Out. I guess he's sorting footy stuff.'

It's okay. He'll be back tomorrow and I'll bake him Monte Carlos.

I'll talk to him about football. I'll talk to him about the mainland.

I'll make him smile.

# CHAPTER SIXTEEN

In the hallway before school our fingertips brush as we pass each other.

I knew he'd come back.

At lunch time, I give him the biscuits and a new Paddle Pop—rainbow this time.

'Thanks, Champ,' he says, and it doesn't bother me that he calls me that. 'And I've got something for you.' He reaches into his backpack and my heart begins to thud.

*It won't be a flower. It won't be a love letter. Shut up, Tiger. You and your stupid hopes.*

It's not a flower, nor a love letter. Wally pulls from his bag a folded pile of brown and gold.

I shake my head as he hands it to me. 'What? No. Wally, that's your guernsey. You need it. It's your lucky one.'

Wally shrugs. 'I thought you might like it.'

He drops the guernsey on my lap and nods. 'And look.'

I unfold it, hands trembling. On the back, he's written a fragment of a poem. I recognise it from English class. It's Robert Frost, I think. I squint, trying to remember how the rest of it went.

'What's this one called?' I ask him. 'I know it, but ...'

He just smiles. 'There's another message, too,' he continues. 'Inside. But you're not allowed to look at it now, okay? Look at it alone. Promise? In, like, a week. Look at it then.'

I nod. 'I promise.' I'd promise Nick Wallace anything. I'd walk into the sky for him.

I'm fighting back tears. *He thinks I'm awesome.*

'You're sure?' I ask Wally. 'You want me to have it?'

'It's all yours,' he says. And then he leans in. 'Don't get all emotional on me, you. Life is beautiful. Just smile, okay?'

I wonder when we'll kiss again.

'So, um, you'll probably need a different guernsey, anyway,' I say, tentatively, 'when you're playing on the mainland? That's why, right?'

I expect to see that ocean grin again. But Wally's face darkens a bit. He shrugs and turns away.

'Pete, I got you something too.' He passes over a pair of footy boots—brand new. 'They were a pressie from my nan,' he says. 'Don't fit properly but they're a good brand.'

'I know,' says Peter, turning them over in his hands. 'They're wicked and, Wally, they're worth a stack of money. You could sell these. They're wasted on me, mate. You know I suck. I'm never gunna make the team. I'm just a "nerdy, delusional ranga", according to Pedda. I don't deserve your boots.'

'Pedda's a dickhead,' says Wally. 'You're getting better. I reckon next year you'll make the team, for sure. Especially with these babies on. Keep trying, okay, for me? And don't worry about the boots. I just did a clean-out of my room, that's all. I have so much junk I needed to get rid of. It's nothing, honestly. Just take them and, you know, bloody practise a bit, hey? You'll never get better if you don't practise. Spend less time pretending to be Austin Powers, more doing drills and you'll be a Hawk in 2019, no worries. Okay?'

'Who's Austin Powers?' Peter asks.

'He means, stop pretending to be Lech of the Century,' Mel says, 'because you're fooling nobody and Pedda still won't give you the time of day.'

'I *mean*,' Wally says, 'you deserve the boots. Just, you know, do them justice, okay? Put in the time.' He winks at Mel. 'And, yeah, just try and be yourself a bit more, okay? Before you give Melody a stroke.'

Peter winks. 'Okay. Cheers, mate.'

'And hey, Rozza, Mel? Got stuff for you two as well.'

'What's up with you, idiot?' Melody growls, her eyes narrowing. 'Having a quarter-life crisis? Going for a life of minimalism?'

Wally chucks her a beaten-up book. On its cover there are two girls sitting on a trapeze.

Melody peers at it. '*Tipping the Velvet*?'

Wally shrugs. 'When we first became friends, I'd never met a gay girl before. I didn't really … understand. I asked Mrs Kuzmic in the library if there were any books about, you know, lesbians.' To Wally's credit, his cheeks don't colour. 'She told me about this one. She said they didn't have it in the library, but I could have her copy. It's awesome. You'll love it.'

'Wow.' Melody nods, holding the book close to her chest. 'Just … wow.'

I look over at Roz, who's standing awkwardly, one foot wrapped around her other calf. 'You honestly don't have to give me anything, Wally,' she says. And I know why she's embarrassed. Roz hates it when anyone gives her gifts. Her family is so rich, they can afford to give her anything. She hates us spending any money on her, when none of us have as much as she does.

'It's fine, Roz,' Wally says, gently. 'I want you to have it.' He passes her over a plastic bag. It's got clothes in it, too, like my present. But hers isn't a guernsey. It's a t-shirt. She laughs when she sees what's printed on it.

'Screw the system.'

And a picture underneath of a cartoon girl flipping the bird.

'This is yours?' Roz asks. 'I never saw you wear it.'

Wally shakes his head. 'Nah. Got it for your birthday. I just decided to give it to you early.'

Roz's cheeks are bright pink. 'This top is made for someone like Mel. Not me. I don't know if I'm brave enough to wear it.'

'You are,' Wally says, simply. 'If you really like it?'

'It's perfect,' she sighs. 'It's so, so perfect.'

Wally's smile is huge. He nudges me with his hip and winks.

I wonder when we'll kiss again.

He's still so close to me. I can feel the warmth of his body.

After lunch, I wave goodbye to him and he salutes me.

I wonder when we'll kiss again.

Dear Dad,
This is the last one.
Should I just burn them?
Let the ash fly away ...

# CHAPTER SEVENTEEN

I'm on Express checkout next to Rhino. He's in great spirits, serenading me between customers—The Backstreet Boys and 5ive—and drawing me silly pictures on the receipt roll stubs.

I'm wearing the guernsey, under my work shirt. It's my secret.

I draw Rhino a unicorn with some sparkly eggs. He tells me they're cool and, one day, we should go on a unicorn hunt together. Then Jamie comes over and 'confiscates' my picture of the unicorn from Rhino to show the manager, and then goes and hides behind the loo rolls.

The next customer who comes through my checkout has to ask if I'm okay because I'm cry-laughing so hard.

When I knock off, at a quarter past nine, I'm surprised to see Auntie Kath's beetle parked out front. Usually, I get a lift home with Rhino's mum and dad on Tuesday nights.

Rhino's parents are here, too, and Auntie Kath is standing by their car, talking to them through the window.

She looks up as we approach. Her face is grey.

My first thought is Granda Craig and Grandma T.

'What's wrong?' I yell, speeding up. 'Is it Grandma T? Is she sick? Or Granda Craig? Did he fall in the paddock or something? What happened?'

Auntie Kath shakes her head, slowly, and I see there are tears in her eyes, shimmering under the fluoro lights in the car park. There are tears on her face, too. She's not bothering to wipe them away.

Her hands reach for me. She rubs my arms. Her chin is trembling.

'It's not Mum and Dad, Tiger,' she says. And that's when Mabel's passenger door opens and Grandma T climbs out. She strides over to me and pulls me into her. Holds me so tight I feel like I'm being squeezed to nothing.

I know I should feel relieved, but my chest feels strange and hollow.

'What's—' I begin, pulling back from Grandma T's shoulder.

'Tiger, it's Wally,' Auntie Kath says. Grandma T lets me go and now Auntie Kath has her arms around me.

'Honey,' she says again, into my hair. She takes a deep, shaking breath.

'Tiger, Wally's dead.'

Dear Mum,
I fell in love
With a perfect boy
And he was magic, magic, magic
And the wind blew him away
Like a dandelion clock
And I'm breaking, broken,
Brittle and bare and all I am
Is a howl
And my throat is raw with it
There's acid in my tears
And I want to write it to you
Until my fingers bleed
It's not fair
It's not fair
Mummy
I wonder when he'll kiss me again

Nick Wallace is
Curly brown hair
Brown eyes so dark they're almost black
Skin like Jersey caramels
Long, thin legs
Rough hands
One dimple, on the left-hand side
Freckles on his nose like cappuccino dust
Broad, lopsided smile
A voice like chocolate
A laugh like sunbeams
Kindness
Gentleness
Thoughtfulness
Nick Wallace is the sky
Seagulls
The ocean
The clouds
Nick Wallace is
Nick Wallace was
Nick Wallace isn't
I am
I am nothing

# CHAPTER EIGHTEEN

The school assembly hall has never been this silent.

Usually, before assemblies, until we're called to order (even most of the time after), the noise in this hall is deafening.

Today, nobody wriggles. Nobody laughs. Nobody speaks.

We wait. Silently. Some people lean their head on the shoulder of their friend. Some people clasp their neighbour's hand so tightly their knuckles turn white.

Some people cry.

But they do it silently. Tears roll from cheeks; splash on Docs and Vans.

Melody sits on my left. Roz sits on my right.

Melody squeezes my hand. Roz strokes my hair.

I do not cry.

I do not move.

My heart seems like the only thing inside me that's alive. It beats furiously, feverishly, as if I'm being chased by a bull or a bear.

Everything else is numb.

He's gone.

He's gone.

*He's gone.*

Why is my heart even beating, still? Why aren't I dead, too?

We all know why we're here. News of Wally's death spread like wildfire; like a contagion. Ms Newall won't be telling us anything that will shock us. There won't be gasps today. Nobody will faint to the floor. We all know exactly how he did it—the rope and the tree. And he fell.

I heard some people murmuring, on the way in, asking, 'Why is there even an assembly? What can they tell us that we don't already know?'

We know everything.

We know Nick Wallace died, alone, in his backyard, while his mum 'ducked out to the shops'.

We know she found him when she returned (with a box of pasta and a bottle of carbonara sauce in a string bag over her shoulder), hanging from the silver birch in their backyard.

His face was blue.

Maybe that's true. Maybe we only imagined it.

We know that Hannah screamed, and that the bottle of sauce smashed on the ground, and her neighbours on both sides came running.

And then the police came.

And the ambulance.

Why an ambulance?

His face was blue. His heart was no longer beating.

Why are we here?

What can Ms Newall possibly tell us that we don't already know?

She climbs the stairs to the stage, slowly. When she takes her place, behind the lectern, she straightens her black cardigan; smooths her blonde hair behind her ears; clears her throat, twice.

Ms Newall is the powerful, polished, professional head of our school community; the youngest principal in our school's history, younger than Auntie Kath. Only ten years or so older than all of us. She has a younger sister in our year.

A younger sister as old as Wally was.

Across the row, I see her sister, Meg, give Ms Newall a little wave and Ms Newall manages a tiny smile.

But then, as she looks down at the papers in her hands, her smile drops.

'Students,' she begins, 'you all know why you are here.'

Nobody makes a sound. Nobody even mutters. *Yes*, we all know why we're here. We stay silent.

She goes on.

'Nick Wallace, a beloved member of our school community, has tragically passed away. Many of you will know the circumstances surrounding his death. I won't go into them again, here. I will only say this, I hope—with every fibre of my being—I pray that you all know that the cause of Wally's ... of Nick's death, is, in my heart, the most devastating way for a life to end. And I pray that none of you out there feel ... or will ever feel, what he must have ...' Ms Newall breaks off. She shakes her head. 'I'm sorry,' she says, quietly. 'I am not handling this well. I wish that I was. I wish I could stand up here and be strong and brave, for all of you, but I'm not feeling strong. I'm feeling ... just exactly how I imagine all of you are feeling. Grief-stricken; devastated; bewildered. I want you to know that I will be seeking counselling, to help me deal with this tragedy. I want you to know that there is no shame in seeking help, if you need it. I do. And we will be offering counselling to every single one of you starting tomorrow. I will be going around your classrooms, personally, to talk with you and to help you make appointments. We will be bringing in extra counsellors to be there for you. Those of you who were close friends with Nick—'

Am I imagining now that she looks straight at me?

'—you, I will be coming to see, right away, following this assembly. You will have priority appointments with one of our school counsellors this afternoon. But if any of you—even those of you in other grades, who weren't close to Wally— feel like you need an urgent appointment, we will ensure that counselling will be provided. We will let you know the details for Nick's memorial and funeral as soon as we can.'

Ms Newall shakes her head again. She takes a small step back from the lectern. Mrs Dennis, the vice principal, takes her arm and offers her a bottle of water. Ms Newall takes a sip, then steps forward again to the lectern. 'I wish I had better words for you today, but the best ones I can give you— the most important ones I want to give you—are these: No matter how bad you feel today, how completely distraught and overwhelmed you may be, how hopeless … please keep hope. Please know it will get better. Everyone in this school community is in this together. We are all here for each other. We can get through this together. You are not alone.'

She blinks back tears and, again, she says, 'You are not alone.'

But it's not true. I have never felt more alone in my life.

'I'd like you all to return to your classes now,' she says. 'It's important that you keep up your routines; that you stay here on school property and attend all your scheduled appointments. But if you need a moment—to laugh or talk or cry—your teachers will allow that to happen. I will see all of you soon and, in the meantime, my door is always open.'

Mrs Dennis takes the microphone then. 'Grade Sevens will exit first …' she begins.

I stand up.

Roz takes my hand. 'It's not our turn yet, Resey,' she says, gently.

'I know,' I say. 'I'm going.'

'Where?' asks Melody. 'We have to go to class?'

I shake my head. 'No.'

'But … Ms Newall said … and you need to make an appointment …'

I shake my head again. 'No.'

And before either of them can stop me, I run down the aisle and out the back door of the hall.

Outside, the sky is an almost insulting shade of brilliant blue.

The breeze is soft. The sun is gentle and mild.

It's all too *nice*.

The sky should be full of clouds and crows.

*He didn't love me. He didn't decide to stay.*

I hear the other students spilling out of the side doors of the hall. I have to get out of here before a teacher spots me.

I break out into a run towards the school gates. I run through them, out onto the road.

I don't know where I'm going. I only know I can't be here.

But I have to be here, don't I? I have to stay. I have to attend my classes. I have to find normal, somehow. I have to go on …

I have to go back.

I slide down the brick wall surrounding the school grounds. I drop my head to my hands.

'Tiger?'

I don't look up. I know her voice. It's the only voice I can imagine wanting to hear right now. Belonging to the only person I can handle seeing me like this. The only person who feels like safety.

Her arms are around me and they're home. 'What are you doing here?' I murmur into her hair.

'If I tell you I've been parked across from the school all day, like a creepy stalker, would that shock you?'

'Not even a tiny bit,' I tell her.

'Come with me, my darling,' she says. 'I'll take you home.'

I shake my head. 'I have to go back. I have to go to class. I just needed … a break. But I'm going back.'

'Tomorrow,' she says. 'Tomorrow, you go back. Today, you're coming with me. You're coming home.'

# CHAPTER NINETEEN

And so Auntie Kath and I sit on the back porch of our house.

I'm bundled up in one of Kath's fluffy dressing gowns. When we got home she made me go straight to the shower ('Everything feels better when you're clean and warm and dressed in something fluffy'). When I came back downstairs, she was pouring boiling water into enormous mugs.

She indicated with her head that I should follow her to the porch.

There was already a tray of biscuits waiting.

'Did you make these?' I ask her, biting into a plump gingernut.

She shakes her head, blowing on her tea. 'No, Tiges. Crusty's at Wivenhoe made those. I'm … not in a baking mood today.'

I take another bite. I know it should taste delicious, but it feels as if I'm chewing chipboard. I put the rest of the biscuit down on the arm of my chair and drink some tea.

For a little while, we sit in silence. I watch a blackbird bobbing about on the lawn, searching for worms; a cat tightrope-walking on a fence across the road.

'Was school … bearable?' Auntie Kath asks me.

'Before I did a runner, you mean?'

I turn to face her. She looks pale and tired. She isn't in her painting clothes today. She hasn't made any art today. She's in wool leggings and a vintage Stevie Nicks t-shirt. Stevie's huge, haunted eyes stare at me through a thick blonde fringe. A black beret sits atop her head. She looks like she *knows*.

But how can anyone really know what it feels to go through this?

How can anyone go through this and survive?

'There are going to be counsellors at school,' I tell her.

'I know,' she says. 'Ms Newall called me. She said she's made you an appointment with Megan Koetsveld tomorrow.'

Mrs Koetsveld is the school counsellor. She's also married to Grace, one of Auntie Kath's friends from uni.

She's lovely, but …

I shake my head. 'No,' I say. 'I can't. I can't talk about it. If I talk about it …'

Auntie Kath nods, slowly. 'I know. I understand,' she says, quietly. 'If you talk about it, you'll fall—'

'Completely apart,' I finish, in a whisper. I look up at her, pleadingly. 'Could you call Ms Newall back and say …'

Auntie Kath looks down at her tea. She puffs up her cheeks and blows out. 'Tiger, I don't know … All the kids are meant to have a session; at least one session. And you were closer to Wally than anyone. They'll be expecting you to …'

Before I can protest, she goes on. 'But I understand, Tiger. We all process this stuff in our own way. When your mum left … it was like grief. It took me a really long time to … well, I'm still not over it. But I was a real mess for a long time. And all my friends said that I should go and see someone, but I just couldn't. For months, afterwards, I pushed them away; got furious at them whenever they suggested it. Finally, I went, though. I saw someone. I talked. And it did help. But I had to go when I was ready.'

'I'm not ready. I just need to …'

Fade away. Be a shadow. Be nothing. Feel nothing. Lock my heart away.

Auntie Kath stares at me for what feels like forever.

She nods. 'I'll call Rachel,' she says, using Ms Newall's first name. Auntie Kath used to babysit Ms Newall when Kath was a teenager. 'I'll call Megan, too. I'll make sure she makes time for you when you decide you need it.'

'Thanks,' I say. And I try and say it in a way that seems okay; a way that seems positive. A way that says, *I will go and talk to Ms Koetsveld soon.*

A way that stops Auntie Kath worrying.

A way that makes it look as if I'm not a tangled pit of snakes inside.

'Melody's mum said that the funeral time has been arranged,' Auntie Kath says. 'Sunday morning. Will you—'

'Of course,' I say, quickly, attempting a smile. 'We'll all go. It's the right thing to do.'

'I'll be there,' she says. And then, softer, 'I'll always be there by your side, Tiger. I'll always make sure you're okay.' The last thing she says, I know, is for herself as much as it is for me. 'It will all be okay.'

# CHAPTER TWENTY

I do up the buttons on my black cardigan.

I brush my hair and tie it back.

I straighten my black skirt.

I pick the balls of fluff from my stockings.

I fasten the clasps on my black shiny shoes. I buff them one more time with the square of sponge.

I make sure my fingernails have no dirt beneath them.

I check there's no food in my teeth.

Auntie Kath made me eat breakfast.

I scan myself in the mirror.

I don't care about the flat chest or the wide belly or the bumpy nose or thin lips.

I care only that I look how I feel inside. No colour, no life, no hope.

The letter he left me said he wanted no tears. It said he wanted people to smile when they thought of him.

I don't care what he wanted.

He left us with no colour.

No hope.

No him.

I don't love him anymore. I can't love him anymore.

They said he wrote letters to his dead dad.

I begin letters and throw them away. I write poems and burn them.

What use is poetry? All it does is show us beauty, but *nothing* is beautiful.

Words are empty.

I check the buttons on my black cardigan.

I pin back the four loose strands of hair.

I straighten my black skirt.

I pick imaginary fluff from my stockings.

I buff my black shiny shoes one more time with the square of sponge.

I make sure my fingernails have no dirt beneath them.

I check that there's no food in my teeth.

Auntie Kath made me eat breakfast. Toast. Jam. Tea.

It is this day. This black day.

'It will be okay,' Auntie Kath whispers.

She takes my hand.

I want to drop it. It feels too tight.

It all feels too tight; too bright; too much.

I want to run.

Dear Mum,
Can you hear me screaming
Wherever you are?

# CHAPTER TWENTY-ONE

Hannah's face is void. There are no tears. None of the howling I expected.

She is empty.

She is like me.

She holds another of his guernseys as if it's a security blanket. I think of his favourite one in my bottom drawer. I don't know if giving it to her will fill the hollow or empty it more.

Or fill it with something that's worse than emptiness.

Melody is on one side of me and Roz is on the other. Peter walks in front of us with purpose. He is wearing the footy boots Wally gave him. He is determined to do what Wally asked in the note.

He's smiling.

Peter's made a mixed playlist of Wally's favourite upbeat songs—everything from Ball Park Music, to John Butler Trio, to Mark Ronson. The priest said it was okay.

Peter's happy for now, because he thinks he's doing what Wally would've wanted, and this makes him feel like Wally's death has some meaning.

We read Wally's note.

We all did.

He said it wasn't our fault.

He said it was to do with dreams.

He said the game the scout came to was the best game of his life.

He said that it didn't mean a thing.

Next week, he might play the worst, or he might never play a good game again, or he might play a hundred great games—but, in the end, what did it matter?

Because the bad games will come eventually. They come to everyone and then what?

Then sixty years of slow descent.

Sixty years of wanting to be with his dad.

He wanted to get there sooner.

He wanted to fall.

*Nothing has meaning,* he said in the note, in his careful handwriting. *Or, if it does, it only has meaning for a small moment. Then it's gone. All you're left with is a guernsey and a pair of footy boots and maybe a trophy or two. Nothing good stays. Everything fades. And that's worse than ending quickly, while people still love you.*

Then he's written out the rest of the poem that was on his brown and gold guernsey. And I know it now. I remember. It's called *Nothing Gold Can Stay.* I remember, now, how when our English teacher asked us what it meant, Wally raised his hand. 'It's all about how nothing—especially things that are perfect and beautiful and magical—can last forever. Most beautiful things only stay for a really short time. That's what makes them so precious.'

*Nothing Gold Can Stay.*

I feel like I might vomit. Because he gave me a clue and I didn't see it. I didn't know the rest of the poem, and I didn't take the time to look it up before … If I had, I could have stopped it.

And I thought that this would be the worst part of his note but it wasn't. Because then he wrote something about me.

*The best kind of person is to be like Champ. Because she is so many things; she'll never fade. She is Champ; she is Tiger; she is Resey. She's everything. She's her smile. And she's knowing that there is something good in the world and it's inside her. I'd rather go now, while I'm still making somebody like Champ smile like that. While she has one magic, awesome, secret memory of me to hold on to. While she still thinks I'm special. Before I'm nothing at all.*

Somehow, everyone in this church knows about the note, even the ones who didn't read it. And I don't know if Melody told or Peter, or Roz or Hannah or even Holland, who read it too. I don't know if he told the boys at practice and they told everyone else.

But I know they know.

Because some of them look at me like I'm golden, and some of them look at me like I'm tarnished, and some of them look at me with pity in their eyes. To them, I'm the girl who was left before she even knew what it was to lose something; I'm the girl who was left again, now I know exactly what it is.

And the rest of them only know there's a secret. They know something happened with Wally. To them, I'm gossip now. I want to kill the lot of them.

I don't cry at the funeral.

I didn't cry when I was left the first time. I didn't cry then for her and I don't cry now for him.

Inside, I'm bellowing.

I'm raging.

I'm not golden and I'm not tarnished.

I don't want to be pitied.

They think what he wrote means he loved me.

He had a choice to stay or go, and if he loved me, he never would have gone.

If he loved me, he never would have written those words that make them look at me like that.

*I hate him.*

The funeral is packed with kids from our school; crying, hugging, wailing, letting it all out.

I will never be able to let this out. It will be inside me forever.

*I hate them all.*

I hate Ms Newall, who squeezed my arm and told me 'my door is open'.

I hate Mrs Koetsveld, who didn't say anything to me, but smiled kindly, sympathetically, and said something to Auntie Kath, which was—I know—about me coming to see her.

I will not come to see her.

I will not walk through Ms Newall's door.

Hannah is empty now. Peter is full of purpose.

I am a shadow. When the sun comes out, I disappear.

And I hate him for it.

# CHAPTER TWENTY-TWO

Emma is at the wake at Wally's house. *Hannah's* house.

She's with her best friends, Katherine and Nicole. She is crying—heaving sobs, shoulders shaking. Katherine is stroking her hair; Nicole is holding her hand. I feel sorry for her.

She still loves him.

Katherine and Nicole lead Emma out of the room and as they do, she catches my eye. She gives me a small nod and I return it.

She knows.

I look across the room to see Hannah talking to Mrs Koetsveld.

Mrs Koetsveld kisses Hannah's cheek, then moves away to talk to some other teachers from school. She's dressed in purple velvet with red resin bangles. She looks as though she thought this would be a different kind of party. She looks how Wally wanted us to look—colourful and happy.

Hannah is dressed in black. She glances towards me. I want to look away. I can't stand to see the hollowness again, but I know I should smile and so I do.

She smiles back. There are tears in her eyes now and—

for some reason—I think this is a good thing.

A light touch on my shoulder makes me stiffen.

I turn. Roz is biting her lip. Melody is by her side, holding her hand.

'Are you okay, Resey?' Roz asks.

'I'm fine.'

They hover like trembling moths. They're uncertain. I'm not acting the way I'm supposed to.

'We need to talk about it,' Melody blurts. 'You need to talk to us. If you won't talk to Mrs Koetsveld—'

'I won't,' I tell Melody. 'And I don't need to. I'm fine.'

'Well, I don't think that's true. You're not fine. Peter's not, either. But at least he's dealing with it *properly*. He had his session … He said it helped a lot. Roz and I went, too. Peter has a follow-up next week because he's still—'

'He seemed fine,' I say. My voice isn't mine.

Or it's the voice of who I am now.

'He's in the bathroom.' Melody's eyes look strange. They don't look like her eyes. Melody Kwong's eyes flash, sparkle, flirt and joke. These aren't Melody Kwong's eyes. Her voice is different, too. 'Bawling his poor little guts out.'

'I'll go.' I say. I don't want to look at those eyes. I don't want to hear that voice.

And I definitely don't want to talk.

'No, we didn't mean you should … You have your own …' Roz is glaring at Melody. 'We can take it, Resey. I said we shouldn't tell you. We can be with him. It's—'

'I'm going.'

I'm already walking towards Wally's bathroom.

*Hannah's* bathroom.

I stand outside and listen to Peter cry.

I put my hand on the door.

I breathe.

I go inside.

I don't say a word.

My eyes stay dry.

I fold him into my arms. 'I thought if I did what he wanted, it would feel better,' he mumbles into my shoulder. 'It doesn't feel better. Fuck him, Resey.'

I don't say a word.

My eyes stay dry.

After a while, Hannah's body is at the door. She sees us, sitting there, curled into each other like a snail and its shell.

'Thank you,' she says. 'For loving my boy.'

Dear Mum,
I don't know if you know about Nick Wallace.
All you need to know is that he's dead.
The funeral is over.
It's all over.
That's it.

# CHAPTER TWENTY-THREE

Except, I keep remembering him.

I'll be doing ordinary things, like cooking dinner or reading my lines, and a memory will hit me like a speeding car.

We are at Jointley's, drawing cartoon footballers on serviettes, making them kick Jaffas through plastic straw goals.

We are on the oval at school, staring at clouds, looking for shapes.

We are ... us.

One summer, between Grades Seven and Eight—a few weeks before school and football and everything that gave our lives their edges—we were all at the beach. We were carefree and wild, itching for our lives to begin again.

Melody and Roz took off their boardies and tee shirts as soon as we arrived and ran into the waves. Peter pretended he was checking his phone, while twisting his arms into muscle shapes to impress the private school girls in their Tigerlily bikinis.

Wally and I sat on the dunes. Just us. I was intending to swim until I saw that Wally wasn't going in. He hadn't even brought bathers with him—he was still in his jeans.

'Not up for a dip?' I asked him.

He shook his head. 'Got a big graze in the final, remember? When Pedda got me with his boot. Swear he did it on purpose, the bastard.'

'He wouldn't do that,' I said, even though I wouldn't put anything past Pedda. He *was* kind of a bastard. 'He's on your side.'

'Pedda's only on one side and that's his own,' said Wally, rolling his eyes. 'Anyway, I gave into temptation last night, and picked some of the scab off. Now it's all raw again and I don't think salt water would be too much fun.'

'Wuss.'

'Yeah, you're probably right. What's your excuse?'

I shrugged. 'Rather talk to you.'

Wally grinned. 'Let's talk. Let's talk about why whales beach themselves or refugees or the US election or—'

'All the fun stuff,' I said, laughing.

'All the *big* stuff,' he corrected me. 'Sometimes, I just need to talk about the big stuff. Otherwise, it gets stuck in my head and I can't get it out.'

'All right,' I said, feeling a little thrill. Wally wanted to talk to me about the important things. The others got football and rock music and school. I got the things that mattered.

He looked down at the sand, drew an infinity symbol with his finger. 'Would you believe I write poems?' he said, quietly. Before I could answer, he hurried on. 'They started off as letters, but they're poems, really.' He shoved his finger deep in the dirt. 'Don't tell anyone.'

He wrote poems. He was funny and smart and an amazing footballer and he had *those eyes* and he *cared* about stuff *and he wrote poems.*

'I—'

Wally patted his belly. 'I'm a starvin' Marvin, Champ. Can we go get some Samboys or something?'

'I'd kill for a Frosty Fruit,' I admitted. 'I'm so hot. But—'

I wanted to talk more about whales and Wally's poems.

I wanted to stay right there with Wally, in this little bubble of us forever.

But Wally stood up and extended his hand. It was rough and hard. A footballer's hand. It felt so good in mine.

And he held my hand the whole way up the beach to the takeaway shop. And we were … us.

Just us.

And I was falling.

Fallen.

He never did show me his poems. He read me other ones. He read me all the poems from all the famous writers.

He never showed me his.

And I wonder now, if he ever really showed me anything of his real self; the Wally beneath the skin, behind the eyes.

Dear Mum,
I'm falling.
Stop me falling.
Didn't you ever think
That this was your job—
To hold me in your arms and stop me
Before I crash?

# CHAPTER TWENTY-FOUR

Auntie Kath sits with me in the car, telling stories of my mum and how she loved me.

'Tell me it again,' I whisper, my head on her shoulder. 'All of it from the beginning. From when she fell pregnant.'

'I always thought it was weird when people said that,' Auntie Kath says. 'Like pregnancy is some Wonderland you reach by falling down a rabbit hole.'

'Tell me about the Wonderland,' I say. I'm tired now. I'm so tired. I want a fairy tale.

But it wasn't a fairy tale, of course. I know that. I know all about my beginning.

I know it began normally. She bought a high chair and a car seat and a change table and booties and little hats and suits that snapped up at the bottom. She was determined to breastfeed; use cloth nappies, not disposables. She carried me during the day in a fabric sling in her arms. She would sleep with me in the bed with her, in a little box they found to make it safe.

She was going to be good at this. Birdie Geeves was good at everything.

Even before her belly got huge, she was practising songs

to sing to me. She was reading stories to the bump.

My dad wanted to know if I were a boy or a girl. She didn't. She wanted the surprise. She told him it didn't matter, anyway. Not all children called 'boy' or 'girl' at birth are really that way. So what did it matter?

At twelve weeks, and then again at eighteen, she bled. My father carried her to the emergency room, crying. He was convinced I was gone. Mum never believed it. She was determined not to fail at this. They called them 'threatened miscarriages'. The ultrasounds showed blood clots in her uterus, bigger than I was and sitting menacingly just above me. If they came loose in one go, I'd fall.

They didn't.

They came loose in small amounts and flowed past me. I hung on, claws gripping hold of the walls of my little home.

They didn't give me a name. She thought she'd know when I came what to call me. She said she couldn't get a sense of me until I was in the world.

At twenty-four weeks she started cramping and bleeding again.

At twenty-eight weeks she went into labour. But I didn't come. Five hours of contractions. Still I held on.

I held on for another six weeks and so did she.

She couldn't fail.

But she was tired.

And I was born—very small, but otherwise strong. I wriggled and writhed in my tiny crib, with the blue lights shining on me.

I was happy. The nurses told Auntie Kath that: 'She's such a happy baby.'

I didn't know she would leave me. I had my mum. That was all I needed.

'Tell me about Wonderland,' I whisper again.

Auntie Kath strokes my hair. 'She sat there for hours in the nursery, with her hand pressed against the glass. Just watching you. She wouldn't let them wheel her back to her room. She didn't want to sleep. She only wanted to be with you.'

But she never gave me a name.

She sat there with her hand pressed against the glass for days, until they let her hold me. She held me so tightly while tears coated her face.

I hold onto knowing that she watched me, waiting to hold me.

I hold onto knowing that, for a little while, she loved me.

Her hand, pressed to the glass.

I hold that tight.

'Is that what you want to hear?' Auntie Kath asks. 'About that time? Is that your Wonderland, Tiger?'

I close my eyes, and it's his face I see, so close to mine. I can feel his breath.

So I don't close my eyes.

'I love you, Tiger,' Auntie Kath says.

And then she cries.

I don't cry.

'Can I put on a CD?' she asks me. 'I could do with some music.'

I nod, my forehead pressed against Mabel's window.

She rifles through her CD folder (Mabel's too retro to have Bluetooth, of course) and extracts a black CD case with a yellow sphere in the middle.

'No …' I groan. 'Coldplay? Really?'

'I listened to this CD all the time when you were a baby,' she says, pushing the CD into the slot. 'It makes me think of tiny you.'

I shrug. 'All right then.'

Chris Martin's plaintive vocals slide out of the car speakers. And I let myself, just for a moment, turn off the part of my brain that tells me I should hate this mournful song. I let myself, just for a moment, mourn. I don't know if I'm mourning Wally or my mother or myself—the old self, before all of it. Because all of us are *done for*. All of us are gone.

# CHAPTER TWENTY-FIVE

Mr Lohrey says, 'You don't have to be here, Therese. We can do other scenes. You won't lose any marks for non-attendance today …'

He trails off. His eyes say everything.

He knows.

They all know. There's a secret. They know I am important in Wally's death. The letter mentioned me. I am part of this.

I look around the chorus. Some eyes are red from crying still, even though I don't know if those kids even really knew him.

In death, they know him. In death, he belongs to them.

They went to his funeral. They clutched those booklets with his picture on the front.

He's not flying. He's tied down here in the hands and heads of all the kids who think they own him now.

But I was the only one he mentioned in the letter. And they all know. I'm supposed to be golden now. And everyone is treating me like I'm breaking or broken.

I don't want that.

I can't be broken if I'm nothing.

'I'm fine,' I tell Mr Lohrey. 'I want to be here.'

Mr Lohrey nods. His voice is gentle and I hate it. 'Whatever you need. It's not a problem to change things. Even if you wanted to go and see Megan? Mrs Koetsveld? She said you haven't been …'

'I'm not going,' I blurt. 'I don't need to go. I'm fine.'

Mr Lohrey nods. 'All right. Maybe we'll start with the dentist song then. Brad?' Mr Lohrey looks over at Brad Petterwood, who has his arm draped over one of the wet-eyed chorus girls. He shrugs. He doesn't care.

'Excellent. Thanks, Brad,' says Mr Lohrey. 'I think that needs the most work. Then Downtown. Does that suit you, Therese?'

I wish he'd stop treating me like I'm about to crack.

'I'm fine,' I say, my voice rising again so it echoes in my ears. 'Can't you see I'm fine?'

Mr Lohrey gives a little nod. 'Sure,' he says, quietly. 'Of course you are.'

A ripple goes through the chorus and moves up towards the stage.

'Look. Look at her. She's so not fine.'

'She's messed up.'

'It's because of Nick Wallace.'

'They were best friends, you know.'

'They must have been more than that. Remember the letter?'

'Do you think they had sex?'

'Do you think she's crazy?'

'She didn't have her session. She wouldn't go. I went to my session.'

'SHE'S CRACKING. CAN YOU SEE HER CRACKING?'

They're wrong.

I don't feel anything at all.

I ignore the idiotic, pitying looks of the chorus as I march past them onto the stage.

I take my broom from a stage hand and I stand in my position: downstage left.

The music starts.

*I am not me.*

# CHAPTER TWENTY-SIX

'Hey, comrades.'

Rhino looks up from his pie and grins. Flo freezes. She opens her mouth, and I know she's going to ask me if I'm okay.

It's my first shift back at work … *after.*

*I am okay. I am okay. I am okay.*

I don't want to have to say it. I want to escape. This is one of the only places where Wally is not. I don't want him here.

Before Flo can speak, Rhino blurts, 'On which side does a tiger have most stripes? On the outside!'

I am okay, so I laugh.

*I am normal. This is normal.*

My heart is in a box. I can't even feel it, anymore. I am a shadow. *I am okay.*

'That's terrible, Rhino,' I say. I sit down next to him and poke him on the arm. 'So. How's tricks?'

'Chillin',' he replies. 'Killin'.'

Flo is looking at us, confused. 'Um, Tiger—'

I shake my head, lips pressed. 'Flo, can … I just want things to be … just like how they always are, okay?'

Flo nods, slowly. 'Okay. That's fine. I get that you don't want to talk. When my nan died the last thing I wanted was to talk about it.'

'I've got another one for you,' says Rhino. 'What's stripy and bounces up and down?'

'Let me guess. A tiger on a trampoline?'

'It's no fun if you guess them,' Rhino says, mock-angry.

'Sorry,' I reply. I'm grinning. I wasn't expecting to be grinning today.

I turn to Flo. 'So, tell me about your day.'

'Seriously?'

I sigh. 'Seriously, Flo. Please. I need normal. You get that, right?'

Flo smiles and squeezes my hand. 'I get that. Right. My day, huh? Okay, so ...' She looks at the ceiling. 'Well, it was pretty cool, actually. I wagged science and walked into town with Allie—'

'Your girlfriend?'

'Ex.' Flo smiles. 'But we're still besties so, like, "goals". Even if she is already seeing Becca Hatami. I'm totally fine. Anyway, we went to Red Herring because she was after some new thongs and—'

'Chloe Hammersmith, service twenty, register five, please. Chloe Hammersmith.' Jamie's voice whines on the PA.

Flo throws her fork into her Tupperware. 'Ye Gods. I swear I could take that kid. I could totally take him and kick his little pimply arse and—'

'Chloe to register five immediately. Chloe.'

'I think he's in love with you,' says Rhino. 'He never calls us like that.'

Flo groans. 'That's all I need. The cyborg love of the Jamienator. Awesome. See you out there, comrades.'

'You go, girl,' Rhino says. And he starts humming a tune. Flo and I look at each other, rolling our eyes.

'"Break My Stride",' we say, in unison.

Rhino begins dancing to his own music, even throwing in a running man.

'You're an idiot, Rhinoceros,' Flo says, but she's smiling.

When she's gone, Rhino turns to me. 'You good?' he says, casually.

I appreciate it. The neutral face. The eyes that aren't full of pity.

'I'm fine,' I say. 'I've got plenty going on. Musical, work, band, school. Keeping busy. You know.'

'Keeping busy with all the boring stuff.' Rhino takes a large bite of his pie and spits pastry as he asks, 'What about doing something fun?'

'I do fun stuff,' I protest. 'I do lots of different things. Acting, singing, clarinet, creative writing, art ... watching footy.'

'Super,' Rhino says, sucking a glob of tomato sauce from his thumb. 'Props to you and your many extra-curricular activities. Your resume must be banging.'

'You're really having a go at me right now?' I snap.

'You said you were fine,' Rhino counters.

'I am.'

'Well, then.' He puts a piece of soggy pastry on his fork, pulls the fork back and catapults the pastry at my head. 'Take that.'

'You bastard!' I pick the pastry from my hair and flick it

back at him.

'You won't be calling me that tomorrow,' he declares.

'Oh yeah and why's that?'

Rhino looks at his watch. 'Better get out there. The Jamienator does not tolerate slackers.' He inclines his head to one side and grins. *'Hasta la vista,* Latey!' he says, mimicking Arnie's robot voice. 'I'll be … hiding behind the bog rolls.'

He laughs at his own bad jokes. I roll my eyes.

'What?' Rhino asks. 'That was gold just there. Comedy gold!'

'Why won't I be calling you a bastard tomorrow?' I repeat, following him to sign on.

'Because, tomorrow, you are not going to musical practice or band or bloody Morris Dancing rehearsal—whatever it is you had planned. Tomorrow, you're going out with me.'

'I can't,' I protest. 'I don't have practice but I promised Melody—'

'Do you want to do whatever it is you promised?' Rhino asks, wiping his greasy-pie hands on his work pants, before pressing his index finger to the scanner.

I think about his question. *Do I want to?*

Melody wants me to come over to her place to 'chat' about my 'pent-up feelings'. She says, if I won't talk to a professional, I have to at least talk to her, because she is practically a professional. She says, if I don't talk to someone it is going to have 'horrendous consequences for your future mental health'.

She says that we should talk 'at least once a week'.

She says it is her duty 'as a feminist to ensure that my friends practise adequate self-care'.

She says that I shouldn't feel like I am imposing on her, because it will be 'excellent practise for my future career'.

She said a lot a more, but I wasn't listening.

And Rhino's right.

I really don't want to go to Melody's house tomorrow.

I really don't want to talk to her. I don't want to be her 'practise'.

And my mental health is fine.

He eyeballs me. 'I know you, Tiger Geeves. And you and I shall be adventuring tomorrow.'

He gives me a little bow as he heads off to the express checkouts.

I'm on register thirteen because it's the nicest one and I'm the broken duckling. I'm offered two breaks instead of one.

Even the customers are nicer.

I wonder if they know.

When an old lady asks me, 'Are you all right, dear?' I put her loaf of bread underneath her milk.

Rhino does stupid dances whenever he catches my eye. He's the only one I don't want to kick in the shins.

Just before the end of my shift, a boy comes in who looks exactly—and nothing—like Nick Wallace.

For a moment, my breath catches. But it's only a stupid moment.

And after it, I'm completely fine.

# CHAPTER TWENTY-SEVEN

But that night, I dream of him.

The dream begins with me sitting on my bedroom floor. I'm alone and my room feels too cold; too small; as if the walls are closing in on me. I climb up on to my bookshelf and push at my bedroom ceiling.

And it flies off into the sky.

I can see clouds through the hole where my ceiling was and miles of empty grey.

Then the sky is all around me.

I'm at the footy ground. I'm still in my pyjamas, but I'm standing in the bleachers of West Park Oval.

And in the centre of the ground is Wally. He's not surrounded by other players. He's alone and he's not dressed in his guernsey, shorts and long socks. He's all in black. And, beside him, there's a fountain. And he's throwing in coin after coin.

*He's making wishes.*

His mouth is opening and closing, but the words forming are muted.

'Wally!' I yell out to him. 'Tell me what you're wishing for.'

He can't hear me, or he pretends not to. He just keeps throwing more coins; making more silent wishes.

I try to run towards him, away from the bleachers, onto the grass. But something is holding me back.

Someone.

I turn and I see that Melody and Mrs Koetsveld, each hold one of my hands. They are trying to drag me away from Wally.

'Let him go!' they yell at me. 'Move on. Let him go!'

I shake them off. I have to get to Wally.

He still hasn't seen me; he's looking at the clouds. Wally raises his arms and I see they're not arms anymore—they're wings. Seagull wings. Then Wally leaps into the air and disappears.

In his place, on the ground, *she* lands. And she has wings, too, but not seagull wings. They're golden.

She's wearing a white hospital gown. The sunlight makes a halo of her long brown hair.

She smiles at me and says something but again, I can't hear it.

Then she's running.

'Don't go,' I whisper. 'Don't go, Mummy.'

And then the whisper becomes a screaming. A howling. I feel as if my insides are pouring out of me all over the grass.

The howling lasts for years before it becomes a whimper. She's gone completely by then.

Or was never there at all.

I wonder when she'll kiss me again.

And then, from the sky, comes rain.

Only it isn't rain, really. It's hundreds and hundreds of

pages, and on every one of them, written over and over, are the words:

*Dear Mum.*

*Dear Dad.*

When I wake, the light feels like paper cuts.

# CHAPTER TWENTY-EIGHT

'But I was going to make us dinner,' Melody says, looking confused. 'I had a recipe all picked out. One of Mum's—beef noodle soup—and I thought I could make some sticky rice for dessert. I've been reading more, too. Mum's textbooks. About dealing with grief. And I took heaps of notes after my session with Megan. I'm all organised. Why are you bailing, Resey?'

I shrug; try to sound casual. 'I just forgot about these plans I had with Rhino from work.'

'Rhino?' She wrinkles her forehead. 'The Indian guy with the big nose?'

'Indian-Malaysian,' I correct.

'Whatever. Why do you have plans with him? Seriously, you can cancel, right? We had plans first. You're coming over to talk about Wally, Resey. You can't just—'

I hold up a hand. 'I *can*. It's not what I need, Melody.' In the background the bell for end of lunch rings. 'Sorry. It's just not what I need. Why don't you go over to Peter's instead? He's the one who needs help.'

'He's back at school today,' Roz says, standing up as I do. 'He seems okay. The footy boys are being awesome to him.

Even Pedda. Way nicer than when Wally was alive. Hey, you remember how Wally—'

'No,' I say, more firmly than I mean to. After all, this is Roz. I never snap at Roz. Roz is the kindest, sweetest person I know, and she gets enough aggro at home. I never want to treat her the way her parents do.

But I'm tired of her going along with whatever Melody says. I'm tired of them both. I'm tired of talking. I'm *tired*.

'I don't want to talk about Wally.' I walk, purposefully, across the grass. 'Not now, not tonight, just … I just don't. Yeah? It's not helpful for me. I just need to get on with it.'

Melody and Roz stop walking; I feel their eyes on me as I march away. I don't want to cry. I don't want to talk.

I just want to go with Rhino to the beach.

And then, tomorrow, I'll go to musical practice; and on Thursday I'll work; and on Friday I'll go to band; and then get my homework done for the weekend.

On Saturday I'll go to the footy.

Just like I always do.

Life has to go on. It went on when I was a baby. It went on when I was three. It has to go on now.

Wally is a memory. Memories can't harm you. They're only thoughts and nothing and empty sky.

Melody cries out, 'I know you're angry, Resey. But you're not angry at us. You're angry at Wally.'

I keep walking.

When I get to the edge of the oval, I start to run.

The rhythm of my feet at first sounds just like his name: *Nick, Nick, Nick, Nick.*

I speed up, so it goes away. So the word changes.

*Angry, angry, angry, angry.*

I run past Emma Houston. She catches my eye. I look away.

*Angry, angry, angry,* my feet say.

'Therese?' Emma Houston calls.

The rhythm changes again, as I speed up.

*Leave me alone. Leave me alone. Leave me alone.*

Dear Mum,
I understand now,
The running thing.

# CHAPTER TWENTY-NINE

Rhino and I are walking in the water, our jeans rolled up to our knees and seaweed wrapping around our ankles. Above us the sky is heavy with stars. Seagulls fight on the beach over a wilted chip. Someone's walking a dog, and they call after it, 'Mulder!', telling it not to run too far.

'Why did you bring me here?' I ask Rhino.

'When was the last time you went to the beach?' he counters.

'I can't remember.' It's a lie. I can remember. I came here with Wally.

'When was the last time you did anything other than practise something or work on something or watch football?'

'I like doing those things,' I say, feeling like a song on repeat. 'They make me who I am. I'm not just one thing. I'm all of those things.'

'You're not just "Tiger"?' Rhino asks.

'Are you just "Rhino"?'

He answers without hesitation. 'Yep.'

'What do you do after school then?' I ask. A wave rises behind me, soaking the back of my jeans. It feels kind of nice. Cool. Tingling.

'Whatever I want,' Rhino says, as the wave reaches him.

He laughs as it soaks him too. 'I don't go much for extra-curriculars. I just do whatever I feel like. Unless I have to—tragedy—go to work. But that's not really too bad, either. I mean, you're there. And Flo. And the Jamienator is amusing and there is my pastry adventure to focus on … But apart from work, nup, I don't do all that much.'

'Your resume must be banging,' I say, laughing.

'I actually don't care,' Rhino says. 'Life is about the things we don't plan, not the things we do.'

*I didn't plan for Wally to die.*

'What do you *say*, though?' I ask, to keep the thought away. 'You know, when people ask what you do.'

'People ask that when you're seventeen?' Rhino looks incredulous. 'Nobody asks me that. They just assume I'm a student. What else would I be at this age?'

'Is that enough? To just do nothing?'

The water is turning from cool to cold now. Rhino feels it, too, and we stride from the waves onto the gritty sand.

'I never said I do *nothing*,' Rhino says, reaching into his satchel and pulling out a towel for me to wipe my legs. 'Is this nothing?'

I shake my head, looking down at the ripples. 'I don't know why you're doing it for me, though. We never really do stuff outside of work.'

And I hope with all my might that he won't mention Wally and the letter and the secret. Because he must know. He has to know. Everyone knows.

'I thought you could do with some time on a beach,' he says, simply. 'And then maybe fish and chips?'

I breathe again.

I can breathe now with Rhino.

'Fish and chips sounds good. I just need to text Auntie Kath.' A thought occurs to me. 'Hey, Rhino, won't your girlfriend mind you taking me to the beach and out for dinner?'

Rhino shakes his head. 'Nope.'

'She must be awesome. The girl who has your heart.' I smile at Rhino.

He looks away. 'She is awesome,' he mutters. 'The girl who has my heart.' He elbows me. 'Now go on. Text that rad auntie of yours, so we can get going. I swear my stomach is about to stage a revolt.'

So I send Auntie Kath a message and she sends one back, saying, 'Have fun, Tiger!' Then, we walk together to Fish Frenzy, and eat flathead and beer-battered chips. Rhino tells me all about the rivalry between nineties boy bands, The Backstreet Boys and N'Sync.

His voice is like a lullaby.

# CHAPTER THIRTY

Auntie Kath is still up when I get home, working on a sculpture, listening to 'No Doubt'.

'How did it go?' Her gaze drifts down to my jeans. 'You're wet.'

'I walked in the water,' I reply.

Her face drains of blood.

'With Rhino,' I say, quickly, because I know what she's thinking. We read Virginia Woolf together not long ago. 'It's okay, Auntie Kath.' I put my hand on her arm. 'It's okay.' She nods. She looks hopeful but not convinced. 'It was bloody cold, though,' I go on. Talking normally. Being normal. 'I might actually take a shower—'

'Have you thought any more about talking to Megan?' she calls after me, as I walk towards the bathroom.

'I'm fine,' I call back.

After I'm showered and in pyjamas, I open my box and I put inside it a shell and a piece of driftwood. They're memories of an adventure. And they show that there's more to me than school and work. I think she'd be proud of that.

I try to concentrate on homework—maths and science. My least favourite.

But then I think of Rhino, and how he reckons life comes before homework. And I do something that I haven't done for ages.

I set up my easel, in the corner of the room, and I start painting.

I think of her as I paint: in her floral blouse, speckled with blue and white and red. I think about how she was so many things.

I paint a unicorn and an elf.

I write below them in curlicues:

*Run with me*
*To faraway places.*
*Breathe in the sky,*
*And fall.*

When I go back downstairs for some juice, Auntie Kath is still working. She has a glass of cider now and the music has changed to some early nineties ska.

'Was she clever?' I ask. 'I mean, like, was she a square at school, like I am?'

Auntie Kath sets down her chisel. 'She was,' she says, slowly. 'When it suited her. Why? Are you having trouble with your homework?'

'I'm not actually doing my homework,' I admit. 'I'm painting.'

'Always doing something, aren't you?' Auntie Kath shakes her head. 'You never stop, do you, little Tiger?'

'I do,' I protest. 'I'm stopped now. You're not stopped.'

Auntie Kath wipes her hands on her jeans. 'Now I'm stopped. Want a bickie?' She takes the biscuit tin from the top of the fridge. It's full of the ANZACs we baked together.

Mine are amber-coloured and chewy. Hers are pale and tough.

She forgot the golden syrup.

I take one of my biscuits and one of hers (so she doesn't feel bad), and we walk together to the couch.

'Tell me more about her at school,' I say.

I lean my head on Auntie Kath's shoulder and she tells me how my mum hated maths, but was good at art and English and photography and philosophy. She won awards. She had her photo in the paper. But she nearly failed Grade Ten science.

'She said she hated it and didn't see the point of it, if she was going to be an artist. She only passed because your grandma did half of it for her,' Auntie Kath says, laughing. 'You should've heard the argument, though—a daughter of Therese Geeves, failing at science!' She shakes her head. 'But then, in Year Eleven, just to prove she could do it, she took biology and physics and she aced them, without Grandma T's help. She wanted Mum to know that she could be good at science, if she tried. Birdie could be good at anything if she really set her mind to it.'

'She was brilliant.'

Auntie Kath nods. 'She was the brilliant one. I always did well, but not remarkably.'

'You're a remarkable artist.'

Auntie Kath rolls her eyes. 'Years and years of bloody hard slog have made me a passable artist—'

'Remarkable,' I correct her, firmly, gesturing to the sculpture—the awestruck, ecstatic face beginning to emerge from nothing. Auntie Kath can make magic from emptiness. She is remarkable.

'Yeah, well …' she mumbles.

'You have pieces in the National Gallery in Melbourne,' I remind her.

'And one in London; two in Spain …' she concedes.

'If it wasn't for me, you'd be internationally famous,' I mutter, looking down at my paint-splodged hands.

'If it wasn't for you, I wouldn't have a heart; wouldn't have even a tiny wafer of the happiness I have now,' she says, gripping my arms. 'Don't you ever start to think I'd be better off without you. Don't you ever.'

She shakes me so hard that tears spring to my eyes.

'I'm sorry,' she says, letting me go. 'Did I hurt you?'

I shake my head, blinking back the wetness. I will not cry.

'Tiger—'

She has that look on her face again.

'I should go back up,' I say. 'I should finish my science work. Oh, and tomorrow I have an extra practice for the musical. And I did actually say yes to another shift and—'

'See? You never stop,' Auntie Kath says, again. Her brow is furrowed. She bites her lip.

'I did stop,' I remind her. 'I went to the beach tonight.'

'Good.'

And maybe she thinks I'm too far away to hear the next thing she says, but I do, and it makes me shiver.

'Please stop, Tiger. Please don't run away from me.'

Dear Mum,
You got it, didn't you?
If you keep moving,
Nothing can ever catch you
Long enough to drag you down.

# CHAPTER THIRTY-ONE

I avoid Melody and Roz at school. I avoid Mrs Koetsveld. I volunteer in the canteen at lunch times instead, even though it's not my month.

Nothing is empty. Every minute is bulging.

I write about my days and I put them in my box.

I don't look at Wally's guernsey stuffed in my drawer. I don't think about him.

When I walk the rhythm never has his name.

Sometimes I dream about him, but in the dreams he's dead. I wake sweating and shaking. But it's better, somehow, to dream of him like that.

On Saturday I go to the football. I'm alone. Melody and Roz aren't there, because I didn't tell them that I was coming. When I line up for coffee I'm served by a lumberjack-bearded boy in a fedora, not the blonde girl. I wonder if Melody would have come today if the blonde girl was working. I wonder if she only ever came to flirt with her.

I wonder if she ever cared about Wally at all.

I'm not here for Wally.

Peter comes but he sits behind the interchange, chatting to the players. He waves and nods. I wave back and smile and then I'm alone again.

Some of the footy fangirls walk past and they say, 'G'day'. There's pity in their eyes.

*I don't care. I don't care. I don't care.*

I'm just here to watch the football because it's one of the things I do. Going to watch the football is part of me.

At half time, they have a minute silence for Wally.

Outside, I'm quiet, because it's how I'm meant to be.

Inside, I'm screaming, *Stop it. Stop it. Stop the quiet. Fill the world up again.*

It ends.

I breathe.

I see Hannah sitting behind the interchange too, but further back from Peter. I wonder if she'll keep coming to the games.

Her photo was in the *Advocate* yesterday. Her eyes were red and she held a pair of Wally's footy boots in one hand, a picture of him in the other. The headline read, *Mother and Town Grieving Over Golden Son's Death.*

At the bottom of the article there were a bunch of numbers for Lifeline and Headspace and Beyond Blue. I stared for a long time at the numbers; memorising them. Not because I will call any of them. Just because it was something to do with my brain.

I'm glad the numbers are there. But I don't need them.

The Hawks win, and they say it's for Wally. I wonder, if he were alive, if he'd even be playing today.

Maybe he would have gone already to the mainland; spirited away to train for the draft and next season.

I wonder if he would have asked me to go …

*Stop it, stop it, stop it.*

My feet scream it as I walk away. Run.

I go to buy a meat pie to eat while I wait for the bus.

When I get to the gates Rhino is there, waiting for me. He nods at my pie. 'Classic beef?'

I nod. 'With barbecue sauce, though. Living on the edge.'

'I had a curried scallop one,' he says. 'From Banjo's. While I was waiting for you.'

I walk towards the bus stop. I need to finish my pie before the bus arrives, so I take a big bite. I talk through pastry and mince, not caring. I don't have to care with Rhino. 'Why are you waiting for me?'

He does a funny little shuffling dance; starts humming a Jamiroquai song. I raise an eyebrow. He stops dancing. 'I thought you might be going home to do homework.'

I swallow. 'You thought right. And then I'm baking banana bread with Auntie Kath. And then I'm going over to Brad's house to run through some songs for the musical with him and Jarrod. And then I told Melody I'd—'

'You're not doing any of that.'

I take another bite of my pie while I think what to say. I ignore Rhino's raised eyebrow, his tapping foot, while he waits. 'Yes, I am,' I answer, finally. 'That's the plan.'

'Plans change.'

I shake my head. I see the bus trundling towards us, slowing as it reaches the stop by the park. I ferret in my pocket for my Green Card.

'Why are you doing this, Rhino? The beach and now this?'

'You don't want to do homework. And, right now, you don't want to be with Melody.'

'She's my best friend. And my other best friend died, remember?'

He nods. 'Yes. You can talk about it, if you want. I'll listen forever.'

'I don't want to talk.'

'You don't want to hang out with Melody, either, do you? So I'm giving you an out that doesn't involve more bloody homework.'

'They want to talk,' I admit. 'I want to keep moving. It's the best way.' I bite my lip. 'I should still, you know, do stuff with them. And I will, just as soon as I've … I dunno. As soon as I …'

'When you're ready.'

'Yeah. And I know that I should be handling—'

'Should, should, should.' Rhino takes my arm as the bus pulls up. I let the people behind me—happy people in brown and gold, and grumpy ones in white and red—climb on to the bus before me. '*Should* do homework. *Should* go out with your friends. *Should* get on that bus … Don't get on there. Homework can always be done later and I'm sure that Kath can bake without you.'

'No, she can't. That's the point. She's terrible. She'll make Pavlova without eggs or apple cake without apple. She'll burn the house down. Because her brain is on fire and brilliant and she gets distracted in the middle of baking by ideas for art that will break your heart. And homework can't wait today because I'm already behind.'

'*Are* you behind? Or have you done it all, but just want to spend more time perfecting it?'

How the hell does he know that? How does he know all

this? All the things I thought I was hiding.

'It's got to be good,' I say, sticking out my chin.

'Who says? Besides, I'm sure it's already good. You could do "good" in five minutes, couldn't you, Tiger? And if Auntie Kath stuffs up the banana bread, the Earth won't stop spinning. The world won't break if your plans change, Tiges.'

Plans changed. Wally died.

But if I keep moving, I can outrun the breaking parts. Miss the cracks, like in one of those old Indiana Jones films that Auntie Kath loves.

'Why are you doing this?' I ask again, as the last of the other footy supporters climbs up the steps. 'And don't just say that you're giving me an excuse. What's in it for you?'

'I just feel like it,' Rhino says, simply.

'And you always just do what you feel like?'

Rhino grins. 'Yup.'

I sigh. 'So what do you feel like doing now, Ryan Abdul Haqq Krishnappan?'

'Park,' Rhino says. 'Swings. Possibly slide also.'

'I haven't been on the swings since I was a kid,' I say.

Rhino laughs. 'You still are a kid, Tiges. You've just forgotten it.'

# CHAPTER THIRTY-TWO

On the swings, Rhino insists on pushing me higher and higher, until my shoes fall off and a little girl starts to cry because she's worried I might fall.

'He's a good swing-wrangler,' I whisper to the little girl, whose name we find out is Amelia, when she looks dubious. 'And a great person. You will be safe with him.'

Rhino pushes Amelia for half an hour. She stops crying quickly, and starts laughing and yelling, 'More, more!'

While Rhino plays with his tiny new friend, I chat to her mum, Samantha, about school and her work at a call centre and her other daughter, Charlotte, who's having her first play date without her mum.

'She's my baby and she's growing up too quickly,' Samantha sighs. 'Life's far too short, isn't it?'

I just nod.

She asks me about what I like to do. I tell her about school and band and work. I tell her I like football and baking with Auntie Kath and acting and art.

'And going on swings,' Samantha says.

'Yeah,' I laugh. 'And going on swings.'

'I think going on swings sounds like the most fun part,' she says.

After Amelia has finally tired of swinging, tired of the park, tired of *everything* ('Come on, kidlet, time for your nap'), Rhino and I go to visit the emus.

We laugh at the funny, honking, almost-mooing sound they make, and their Mick Jagger walk.

'Those birds have got serious swag,' Rhino says.

Then we go and sit on the playground train, eating jelly snakes and telling tiger and rhinoceros jokes.

I leave Rhino at the bus stop. 'See you Tuesday,' I say. 'At work. Unless you kidnap me again.'

'Can I kidnap you again?' Rhino asks.

I laugh and shake my head. 'I have to go to musical practice on Monday. And tomorrow I have to catch up on homework. And, besides, aren't you sick of me already?'

'A bit,' Rhino says. 'But, you know, I feel like I'm performing a public service here.'

He grins at me as he waves down his bus. 'I forgot to ask you before, Tiger. How's tricks?'

'Right now, okay,' I admit.

'My work here is done,' he says, boarding the bus. 'See you on Tuesday.'

'See ya,' I reply. Then I think of something. 'Hey, Rhino!' I call out. 'Maybe you can bring your girlfriend next time we go out. I'd like to meet her.'

He mustn't hear me. He's already halfway up the bus. He smiles and waves, while I make a mental note to ask him about his girlfriend again on Tuesday.

I don't even know her name.

I'm home in time to bake. Auntie Kath doesn't ask why I'm late, and she doesn't hassle me to do my homework. She knows I'm on top of it.

We mash banana, sift flour and grease tins. She's concentrating on getting the measuring right; on not forgetting any ingredients; on the difference between stirring and folding.

I'm happy with the quiet. I'm not in the mood for talking.

When our baking is in the oven we sit on the floor, watching it rise. She kisses me on the head and there is silence and warmth and I feel only a few miles from happy, instead of continents.

Outside, the wind is coming up. From one of the branches in the ghost gum across the road, a rope dangles. It was a kid's swing once, until the tyre fell off.

I know that.

But I still have to look away.

# CHAPTER THIRTY-THREE

Melody corners me by the lockers.

'What is going on with you?' she cries. 'I haven't seen you in days—pretty much since the wake—and I'm worried. Roz and I are both really worried. We're worried you're withdrawing. And you still haven't been to your session. I know you haven't, even though when I asked Mrs Koetsveld about it she said she couldn't tell me. And I have a week's worth of pork buns and dumplings and all sorts of fried desserts that my mum's made for you in my locker. And I just finished reading this awesome book by Clementine Ford, and I'm *dying* for you to read it, so we can discuss it. And ...'

Melody looks, suddenly, very small. And Melody Kwong is six-feet tall. She never looks small. 'Resey, I can sort of handle just filling up my Twitter feed with hashtags about how awesome the book is. And I can almost handle the pork smell in my locker too. But I can't handle you not talking to me. Because it's not fair. It really isn't. We've been friends for so long, and I tell you everything, and you tell me everything, and I can't handle that not happening. Please, Resey. I need to talk to you. And you need to talk to me. If you won't talk to anyone else, you at least need to talk to me. Because Wally mentioned you in the letter and I know something happened and I want you to tell me. You're meant to tell me everything. And there's this quote in the book that goes something like feminism helps to feel like a girl and for it to not hurt. And that's true for me, too, but you know what makes it hurt even less? You. You make everything hurt less, Resey, and now, without you, everything just *aches*.'

Melody stops and breathes, finally.

'Are you finished?'

Melody shakes her head. 'No. I also need to tell you I have a new girlfriend and I think I love her.' She pauses. 'Now I'm finished.'

'You have a girlfriend?'

Melody nods and flashes a tentative smile. 'The girl from the coffee stand. Jacinta. JC. She's a barista, and a dancer.' Melody does a half-hearted version of jazz hands. 'I talked to her at the wake and she asked me out. She even skipped a shift so we could have lunch— and omigod, Resey, she likes Roxane Gay. And *Wonder Woman* and she knows all the words from all the musical episodes of *Buffy* and she's planning to study psychology at uni too and … Resey, do you think I did a bad thing? See! I have to ask you this stuff! Was it wrong we got together at the wake?'

I sigh. 'Probably. But I'm happy for you.'

'I'm happy, too,' says Melody. 'But only sort of. Because I can't be one hundred percent happy if you won't talk to me. I need you to tell me the secret that—'

My fingers curl. 'It's not gossip, Melody. I'm not gossip.'

'I know, but—'

'I told you I don't want to talk.'

'Why not? It's not healthy, Resey. You must know that.'

I take out my English books and slam the locker door shut again. 'It's healthy. It's normal. It's fine!' I yell. 'Your way is not the only way, Melody. Surely your feminist books taught you that? There's no one way to do anything, so just let me do things my way. Okay?'

Melody's eyes widen. I don't think she's ever heard me raise my voice before, besides when I'm getting stuck into the umpires.

'I'm sorry,' I say, more quietly. 'I'm sorry I talked to you like that and I'm honestly stoked you have a girlfriend, especially one who likes *Buffy*. I don't care at all where you met her and I want you to be happy and I'm glad you are. And I'll read the book, I'll even eat the buns, but … Melody, I'm sorry, but I just can't be around you right now.'

Melody looks stung. But then she puts on her professional face. 'Because you're not coping with Wally's death.'

I'm coping fine.

*He was hanging in a tree.*

I close my eyes.

I open and close my fingers. I try and breathe, but my lungs feel too small.

Into the bubble I'm making around me, Melody's words pierce like a needle. 'Do you remember when you first saw Wally?'

Grade Seven.

Home Group.

Miss Newman at the front of the classroom, telling us we're all going to be great friends.

Birds at the window.

The smell of grass—it's still summer.

Melody on one side. Roz on the other.

Protected.

My books spread out in front of me, neatly sharpened pencils, new biros, rubbers that smell like strawberry.

Ignoring the whispers from the few kids who didn't know me:

*'Is she the one?'*

*'The one who ...'*

*'She was just a baby.'*

*'I heard it from my mum.'*

*'I've seen her around town.'*

*'That's definitely her.'*

*'Can we ask her about it?'*

*'Do you think she'd tell us?'*

Melody passed me a sherbet bomb and a sticker with a feminist fist on it. *Stay strong,* her note commanded. Roz passed me a fancy artisan chocolate she'd sneaked from her mother's drawer. *We've got you,* hers said, with a heart and a kiss.

I passed two notes: *Thanks, guys.*

*They'll get over it,* a note came back, from Roz. *They used to whisper about me because of my hair and because my parents are rich.*

*They whispered about me because I'm Asian and gay.* Melody winked at me as I read her note. *Let me kung fu their butts. Then we'll talk about it and you'll feel better.*

I knew it was a joke. The kung fu part, anyway. Melody hates martial arts as much as she hates all sports.

The other kids didn't know that, though.

Miss Newman was telling us how to read our timetables.

'Here is first period—it's always a core subject. Core

subjects are Maths, English, Science, Phys Ed and—'

That's when the door burst open.

A flurry of dark curls, tanned skin, long legs.

A brown-and-gold scarf.

*A new kid.*

And, of course, we were all new kids; fresh from primary school, new to this class and to this high school. But most of us had gone together to the same feeder primary school. I would have assumed he was from out of town, but he did look familiar. Like maybe I had seen him, once or twice, out of the corner of my eye.

'And you are ...' Miss Newman was trying to sound tough. Even then we knew she wasn't capable of it.

'I'm Wally. Nick Wallace. I went to the Christian school for primary school, but I moved here for high school for the footy team. Theirs sucked. Pleased to meet you.'

He held out a hand.

My heart changed rhythm; started dancing.

Miss Newman took his hand and shook it. 'Pleased to meet you, too, Wally-Nick Wallace, the footballer. And why are we ten minutes late to our very first class of high school?'

'Would you believe "kidnapped by aliens"?' Wally asked. We all laughed.

Everyone was falling in love with Wally already.

Even Miss Newman. She laughed, too. 'I would like to, because I'm sure it's much more interesting than the real reason.'

'Sadly true, Miss Newman,' Wally said. 'The real reason is that my mother had a bit of a moment in the car park. *Her little boy going to high school.* She got all teary. And then she wanted me to wear a scarf and I said it wasn't on the uniform list, but she got it in her head that I'd be safe from potential germs and contaminants if I wore a scarf.' Wally sighed. 'And so here I am. With scarf. But, hopefully, germ-free'

'You'll need to take off the scarf,' Miss Newman said. 'Even though I approve of the colours. Hawks fan?'

Wally nodded. 'AFL and TFL. I'm going to play for both of them one day.'

'Well that's a great ambition,' Miss Newman said. 'But first you need to learn to read your timetable. We've finished "Home Group". We're up to "What is a core subject?"—it's fascinating stuff. There's a spare seat there.' Miss Newman pointed to the desk in front of us. The one next to Peter.

'Thanks, Miss N,' said Wally, unwinding the scarf from his neck.

'You have one minute to get to know the people sitting next to you,' Miss Newman said. 'Then I want your full attention. She clasped her hands and watched, expectantly.

'Hi, I'm Peter.' Peter extended a hand. 'Otherwise known as *Casanova Pete.*'

'Really?' Wally said, looking dubious.

Peter sighed. 'Nah. But did it work for me? Even a bit?'

Wally took Peter's hand and shook it, firmly, clapping his other hand on Peter's shoulder. 'Just be yourself, I reckon, mate,' he said.

And then he turned to me and Melody and Roz. 'G'day, I'm Wally,' he said. 'I have no friends here whatsoever. Can I steal you fellas? And can this one have you too?' he jerked a thumb in Peter's direction.

Peter laughed. 'Fair call, mate. Yeah, I'd be up for that.'

'You can both be our best friends forever.' Melody spoke for the three of us. 'Only if Resey can have your scarf, though. She's obsessed. Ridiculously.' She pointed at my school folder, which was covered in brown-and-gold contact.

'It's okay,' I mumbled. 'It's your scarf. It's fine.'

'I have two other ones just like it,' Wally said, passing the scarf over. 'My mum is very into scarves. You can have it if you promise to be my very best friend. Deal?'

I nodded. 'Okay.'

I took the scarf.

It smelled like him.

'Onya, Champ,' said Wally.

I loved him from that moment. I never stopped.

*He was hanging in a tree.*

I breathe, open eyes, be nothing.

'Of course I remember,' I say to Melody. 'What's it got to do with anything?'

'Remember how funny he was and how everyone in the class—'

'I don't want to talk about it,' I growl. I push past her and march away, up the hallway towards my English class.

'You have to talk to someone!' Melody calls out after me. 'You have to talk to Mrs Koetsveld. It's important!'

I ignore her; walk faster.

*Leave me alone. Leave me alone.*

I'm not talking to Mrs Koetsveld ever.

I'm not talking to Melody, either.

I'm going to volunteer in the canteen again at lunch time, and after school I'll practise my musical songs. Tomorrow I'll work out a way to avoid seeing her or Roz for the rest of the week.

I'm not talking about Wally.

I need him to be gone.

Dear Mum,
If there was one word
For my life so far,
It would be
Gone.

# CHAPTER THIRTY-FOUR

There's a text message from Rhino when I finish school on Tuesday.

Let's not go to work tonight.

I reply.

What???

Unless you need the dough.

This is just silly. I hit the green call button.

'What are you on about, Rhino?'

'Hey, Tiger. How's tricks?'

'Confused. Now ... what are you rabbiting on about? What do you mean "let's not go to work"?'

'Shouldn't that be "rhinoceros-ing on"? Hey, why don't tigers like fast food? Because they can't catch it!'

'Rhino, you're completely hyper. Please focus. Work?'

'Work. Right. So, do you need the, like, six bucks fifty we'll make down the mines tonight?'

'No. I don't really need the money but—'

'No "buts". I've got it all figured out. You'll say you have a musical rehearsal you can't get out of—they're not allowed to get angry if it's a school thing—and I'll say I've got gastro.'

'You're going to chuck a sickie? But you know the

Jamienator's got a sixth sense for when people are just bunging it on.'

'Lucky His Droidness is not on today—I checked. So he won't be able to whinge to Mr Blakely—well, you know, *say* he's going to whinge to Mr Blakely, and then hide behind the Sorbent. Plus, gastro's heaps easier to fake than the flu, because you don't have to put on a croaky voice. And it's something you can recover from pretty quickly, so I'll be right to work on Thursday.'

'And what if someone sees us when we're meant to be singing or … spewing?'

'They won't. Because we're going on an adventure far, far away.'

'Rhino ...' I say, warningly.

'Come on. I remember you saying a while back that you hadn't been up to Cradle in ages ...'

'Cradle Mountain? Rhino, that's hours away! And how will we get there?'

'I got my Ps yesterday.'

'What? Serious? You never even told me you were going for them!'

'I wanted to surprise you.'

'That's awesome,' I say. 'Go you good thing! But I'm still not going up to Cradle with you. We wouldn't get back before midnight!'

'So? That's when the elves come out!'

It's the mention of elves that starts to turn me. Rhino's right. It has been a long time since I've been to Cradle Mountain, but in my memories it's magic.

Just like the Otherwhere.

There *could* be elves there.

But ...

'So, I don't know about you but I have a curfew. It's flexible but Auntie Kath worries about me if I don't come home when she expects me. Especially now. And I know she stays up waiting for me to come home, even if she pretends to be asleep when I get there. Rhino, I have to go. I'm going to miss my bus.'

'You're not catching your bus. You're coming with me. Look left.'

I do as he says and I see him, leaning up against a beat-up old Commodore, looking like he's just won a gold medal.

'You were there the whole time?' I say. 'That's just creepy. Stalker stuff, Rhino. Hang on, I'm coming over.'

I press the red button on my phone. As I do, I see Roz and Melody walk out of the science block. They see me at the same time and speed up.

I break into a run. Rhino looks confused. 'You can't be that glad to see me.'

'Get in,' I say, quickly.

'Only if you promise you'll let me take you up the mountain.'

'Okay! Okay! I promise!' I cry, opening the passenger door. 'Now get in and start the engine on this pile of crap!'

'Hey!' Rhino holds up his hands. 'You're not going anywhere in Shirley if you call her such nasty names.'

'Shirley?'

'Manson. From Garbage. Nineties icon. You know? "Only Happy When It Rains", "Stupid Girl", "#1 Crush"?' He starts humming.

'Shut up and drive,' I say, but grinning. I've always wanted to say that.

'Fine.' Rhino slides into his seat and turns the key. The engine splutters to life. He beams at me. 'Oh yeah, listen to that. Sexiest sound in the universe!'

'Rhino, if you don't drive away *right now* ...'

I look out my window. Roz and Melody are only a couple of metres away.

'All right, Tiger,' says Rhino. 'Hold on to your stripes. You and me and Shirley M are going on an adventure!'

I don't look back to see their faces. I don't want to see them scowling or sad.

I just want to escape.

I want to be gone.

# CHAPTER THIRTY-FIVE

When they were twelve they ran away together.

They saved up their Dollarmites money and bought two tickets on the Redline to Launceston. They stuffed their backpacks full of Arnott's Shapes, Samboys and Milky Ways; enough supplies for an adventure.

My mum took my dad's hand and whispered to him, 'Come on. I'm taking you to a place that's a bit like the Otherwhere.'

Auntie Kath had told her that The Cataract Gorge was like something from *Lord of the Rings*, and that some people reckoned it was actually a volcano that would one day erupt lava all over Launceston. There was even a chairlift you could go on that let you fly to the clouds.

They spent their day flying and talking to peacocks and hiding in caves and chasing elves.

At the end of it all, they called Grandma T. They knew if they called my dad's parents, they'd both be in heaps of trouble.

Auntie Kath came with Grandma T to pick them up. Auntie Kath was more than happy to come along if it meant she could stock up on art supplies at Birchalls, and a Kate

Bush cassette tape at Wills. On the way home they all stopped in Devonport for Chinese food. Auntie Kath was glad that her sister had run away because she got to have new music and art stuff and deep-fried banana with ice cream.

And because it made her happy to see my mum happy. It made her happy to see how much my dad was properly in love with her sister. Auntie Kath said that she could tell that night. The boy had fallen hard. It happened that day, in the Gorge.

And my mum was in love with running.

'What are you thinking about?' asks Rhino, as we drive further into the wilderness.

'My mum and dad,' I say, without thinking.

I assume he knows.

Everyone in this town knows.

'There's a poem,' he replies, his eyes never leaving the road.

'I don't want to hear any poems,' I snap.

He ignores me. 'I had to read it for school. Our teacher thought he was being so cool, letting us read it, because there's swear words in it. But anyway, it's all about how our parents … well …'

'I think I know the one,' I interrupt, because he's turning red, and because I don't want to hear him say it. I don't want another boy reading me poetry. I don't want another boy telling me lies. 'It's all about how they damage us. Hand down all their flaws and neuroses to us.'

Rhino nods. 'Without meaning to, I guess, because they're just humans, too, trying to work it all out.'

'There's a song Auntie Kath loves,' I go on. 'It makes her

cry. Mike + the Mechanics?'

Rhino holds up a finger. He shuffles the tapes that fill the centre console. He plucks one out. It's a mixtape, with a hand-written card in the plastic cover. He pushes it into Shirley's dusty cassette player. The song is from the perspective of a son, expressing his regret that he never resolved the conflict with his father before he died. It talks about how each generation of children always blames the one that came before it for all our problems. Every word of it is like a knife to the heart.

'Yeah,' I say, my voice sounding hollow. 'That's the one.' I look out the window. Too many trees. A crow flies from the branches of one like a bullet. It bursts through the setting sun and keeps on until I can no longer see it.

'Tiger?'

The song changes to a poppy dance number from the nineties.

'Ah, Culture Beat,' Rhino says. 'The true poets of their age.'

I turn to him, as the verse slides into the chorus. 'Go on, then,' I say. 'Take me away'.

# CHAPTER THIRTY-SIX

I breathe out. I'm a dragon puffing smoke.

It's so cold at the mountain that my toes might've fallen off without me even noticing. I haven't felt them in at least an hour, despite the extra socks Rhino gave me. He brought thick woollen gloves for me, too, and a beanie and scarf and an oversized parka.

Even with all the extra layers, I'm still bloody cold.

But in a good way.

We're walking around the Enchanted Stroll.

We've already seen a wombat's bottom poking out of its burrow, and Rhino is convinced he saw a platypus, but by the time I looked, it had disappeared. 'You scared it off,' Rhino said. 'Everyone knows platypuses are afraid of tigers.'

Now, we're watching a tiny echidna snuffling about in the undergrowth, searching for ants.

'How can an animal with spikes and such a silly long nose be so cute?' I ask. 'And it lays eggs and eats bugs. It's so wrong and yet—'

'It's the perfect crazy combination, I guess,' Rhino says. 'With some people, all the bits just come together to form a perfect whole. And on another person, all those same bits look weird.'

'An echidna's a person now?' I ask, crouching down so I can watch the little creature more closely as it rambles along.

'Uh, did I say "person"?' Rhino smiles. 'I meant "monotreme".'

'Obviously.' I grin up at him.

'Obviously,' he echoes.

'So,' I say, as I look at the sun, plump and sinking happily in the sleepy sky, 'what's your girlfriend up to tonight?'

Rhino shrugs. 'Can't we just talk about echidnas?'

I shoot him a look. 'Trouble in paradise?'

Rhino sighs and looks away. 'Here, I'll make you a deal. You don't mention the girlfriend thing; I won't mention Wally.'

My voice is sharper than I mean it to be. 'Were you going to mention Wally? I thought the whole point of this is so we don't talk about Wally.'

Rhino shakes his head. 'You thought that was … I just thought we were having fun. Why does everything have to be about Wally?'

'He just died,' I snap. 'So I guess, yeah, some stuff should be about him.'

'But I thought you didn't want—'

'Shut up,' I bark.

'Sorry,' Rhino mumbles. 'I'm just confused.'

'You think I'm not?' I try and make my voice gentler. But my forehead is thudding; my hands are clenched into fists. My heart feels wrong in my chest. This all, suddenly, feels wrong. I don't want to talk about Wally. I don't even want to think about him. But Rhino is not allowed to dismiss him.

I know he didn't mean anything by it, but it still felt wrong. He didn't know Wally. He only met him once or twice when he came in to visit me at work.

He is my best friend.

I'm the only one who's allowed to dictate what role he plays in this night. I'm the only one who's allowed to shut him out. Or let him in.

'Sorry,' Rhino say again, quietly. 'I really didn't mean anything by it.'

I shrug. I don't trust myself to answer him.

Above us, a possum screeches.

Rhino's arm shoots out. He hugs me close.

I tense.

'You all right?' Rhino asks, his voice creaking. He strokes my face.

*He strokes my face.*

*'Golden,' he whispers.*

*He doesn't quote poetry; doesn't say another word.*

*He looks like he might cry.*

*I'm filled with stardust. I'm filled with the whole world.*

'I'm fine. You all right?'

'Yeah. Just chillin'. Killin'.'

There's a crunching in the gravel behind us. Rhino's arm drops from my shoulder.

'Evening,' says a male hiker. The lady beside him smiles.

'G'day,' I say, and Rhino says, 'Nice night for it.'

'It's a beautiful night,' she says as they pass. 'The sort of night that makes you believe in love and magic.'

We watch their backs, fading into the darkness.

Rhino begins to hum, softly at first, then more loudly.

'Sorry, weirdo,' I say, giggling as he performs his strange little version of a boy-band dance in front of me. 'I got nothing on that one.' He stops and shakes his head, a disappointed look on his face. '"Could It Be Magic?" Take That?'

'Cheesy.'

'Oh, Tiger. You break my heart!' He presses a hand to his chest, stricken. 'Take That were the seminal nineties boy band. When we get back, I'm going to play you all their old stuff—and their new stuff, too.'

'They're still around?' I'm surprised. Most of the bands Rhino likes disappeared at the turn of the millennium.

Rhino nods. 'Better than ever. How can you not know this stuff? The only way you can possibly redeem yourself is if you tell me you do, in fact, believe in magic. Tell me, Tiger, tell me. I want to know if you believe in unicorns.'

'Of course I do,' I reply. 'They live in the Otherwhere.'

Rhino laughs. 'Naturally. With the pixies.'

'Elves,' I correct. 'Speaking of which, they don't seem to have come out tonight after all. We'll have to try again another night. We really should be getting home. Auntie Kath will be worrying. She'll be listening to baroque pop and painting moody things and glaring at the front door—and only two of those are acceptable. I hate worrying her.'

'How long have you lived with your auntie?' Rhino asks as we walk back to his car. It's only then that I remember: Rhino didn't move to town until he was fourteen. He lived in Hobart before that.

Not everyone in this town knows after all.

'All my life,' I reply, my voice cracking. It's been ages since I've had to talk about this. I've forgotten how. 'For a while, my dad was there. Then it was just us.'

'What about your mum?'

'Gone. Can we add this to the list of stuff we don't talk about?' I'm aware my voice is shaking. My chest feels tight.

We're at the car park now. Rhino opens the passenger door for me and I get into Shirley.

'Like Wally? And your counselling at school?'

I shoot him a look. *Just like that.*

I wish we hadn't started talking like this.

Everything feels gloomy now.

'I have no idea what I'd even talk about if I went for the counselling,' I say, trying for light. 'I have no idea what's in my head, waiting to come out. It could be a dead parrot for all I know.'

Rhino laughs. 'How do you know the parrot is dead if you don't look?'

'It's a cat,' I retort. 'It's Schrödinger's cat that might be dead. Not his parrot.'

'I imagine the same rule applies,' Rhino argues. 'So maybe you should look. I mean, talk, to see the parrot.'

'Don't you start,' I sigh. 'Please.' Rhino turns the key, and Shirley shudders. I hope she manages to get us all the way home.

'I could be there with you,' he says, not taking his eyes from the road. 'I could walk you to your session, wait while you talk?'

When I don't reply he says, quietly, 'It will be okay.'

'Maybe. But it's not okay now.'

Once we're back on the highway home, I try and fix the night. 'Knock knock!'

He laughs. 'Avoiding the D&Ms with knock knock jokes? Sounds like something I'd do.'

'That's not how you reply to a knock knock joke,' I say, sternly.

'Sorry, Tiges. I should know that. Okay, try again.'

'Knock knock!'

'Who's there?'

'Rhino'.

'Rhino who?'

'Rhi-know you're there. Open the door!'

'That sucks, Tiges.'

'I didn't have much to work with, you know? There are heaps more jokes about tigers than there are about rhinoceroses.'

'We're a rare breed.'

'You are.' I look across at Rhino, who's concentrating determinedly on the highway—a senior citizen driver at seventeen. It's the one thing I've ever seen him do carefully. Rhino is wildness, chaos, fun. 'Hey, Rhino?'

'Tiger.'

'Thanks. For tonight. And the beach. And the park. The fun stuff. It's been ... good.'

'Adventures are good,' says Rhino, still staring straight ahead. 'And I'm glad we're having them together. You're cool, Tiger Geeves.'

'You better believe it. But, you know, I don't need a Manic Pixie Dreamgirl episode. I really don't. I can figure this out on my own.'

'I know.' He shrugs. 'I never said you couldn't. We're just adventuring, that's all.'

When we get back to civilisation, we stop for drive-through burgers, chips and ice cream. Rhino grosses me out by dunking his chips in his chocolate sauce. We gossip about work and sing along to Aqua and Eiffel 65 in fits of giggles.

When we pull up at my house there's a moment of awkward silence. It's clear that neither of us knows what to do.

Rhino talks first. 'You'll be okay?'

'Peachy.' I force a smile.

Rhino taps me lightly on the shoulder. 'Don't just sit there …' I raise an eyebrow. I know what's coming. Rhino flashes me a cheeky grin, and then breaks into yet another nineties dance song; this one maybe worse than all the others. I roll my eyes and open the car door.

'Night, Rhino.' He's still singing as I slam the door shut. I can hear tinny music wailing from somewhere deep in the house. As I get closer, it transforms into echoey synths. Enya? Oh, golly. She must be really anxious.

She switches it off as I come through the front door. I hear her trying to move, stealthily, towards her bedroom.

'Auntie Kath?'

Her footsteps halt.

'I was … just getting a glass of water?' she says, guiltily.

I let it hang. She gives a little cough.

'I love you, Auntie K,' I say.

Her voice softens. 'I love you too, Tigesy.'

I go up to my room and I get out my box to put a gum leaf in it for her.

I sit for a while, staring at the box. Trying not to think; trying to be a shadow.

'Bugger this,' I whisper.

I go out into the hall and see there's light coming out from underneath Auntie Kath's door. I knock. 'You still awake?'

'Yep,' comes the answer. 'Just reading a very dodgy novel. Do you need to talk?'

I think about it. 'No,' I say, finally. 'But I could use some cake. You want some?'

Auntie Kath opens her bedroom door. She's dressed in windcheater pyjamas with old-school My Little Ponies on them. 'I couldn't think of anything better,' she says.

Dear Mum,
My friend Rhino says,
Our parents mess up our lives,
But everything does,
Doesn't it?
You're born perfect,
Then, slowly,
Life makes you something else.
Empty
Or rotten
Or sad
Or it makes it so you wish
You weren't alive at all.
I want to go back.
But this time, I want you to hold me
Closer, tighter, longer.
Maybe then I could have stayed perfect.
Maybe everything would have been okay.

# CHAPTER THIRTY-SEVEN

Melody is standing behind the canteen counter, wearing a blue apron.

Melody is not a canteen monitor.

Something very wrong is going on.

'What are you doing here?' I yank my own apron off its hook.

'Volunteering,' she says, raising an eyebrow. 'It's good for mental health. Now, tell me, is it one scoop of ice cream or two in the milkshakes?'

'One and then two squirts of ...' I shake my head. She's trying to distract me. 'Melody, seriously. What are you doing here?'

She shrugs. 'I figured if we're trapped behind a counter together ...'

I sigh. I knew it. It's another ploy to get me to talk.

Thankfully, I have the advantage over Melody. I know that once the shift begins, we'll be so busy making toasties, salad rolls and Milos that talking won't be an option. I look at the clock. Three minutes until the canteen doors are unlocked.

Two can play at this game.

'All right, then. So, I should take you through how to

put the salad sandwiches together.' I move over to the food preparation benches. 'It's not as easy as it looks. And you won't know any of the prices, will you? Hmm, okay, so bags of mixed nuts are fifty cents, and chips and gravy is—'

'Resey, I came early, so I could learn all this stuff. Mrs Butcher's already taken me through it. I know I asked about the milkshakes, but you don't have to—'

'But there's heaps of things Mrs Butcher always forgets to tell you,' I interrupt. 'Like how to clean the tongs and what cycle to put the dishwasher on and how many pieces of beetroot—'

'Resey!'

I glance pointedly at the clock. 'Oh, look at the time. Mrs Butcher, can I open the doors?'

Mrs Butcher peers at her watch. 'Okay, girls. Melody, do you feel confident about your responsibilities here today?'

Mrs Butcher is very serious about her job as canteen manager.

She never *really* forgets about beetroot.

'One hundred percent, Mrs Butcher.' Melody's voice trembles. I look over at her and I'm shocked to see her eyes are red.

Melody never cries.

'Mel?' I say, reaching out for her.

She shakes her head. 'Just open the doors, Resey.'

'Um, okay.'

I unlock the doors. Peter is first in line, surrounded by some of the other footy boys—Brad Petterwood (Petta), Tim Faulls (Faullsy) and Jarryd Groenewegen (Groesey). They're jostling as well as hip-and-shouldering, and I know they haven't always been at the head of the queue. There are some Grade Sevens behind them looking mortified.

'Resey!' Peter says, cheerfully. 'Stunning apron.'

I can't help smiling. I've missed him.

'How's it going, Peter?' I ask, ushering him and the footy boys inside. I let another five people in (including the poor Grade Sevens), then pull the rope back across.

'*Peter,*' Brad says, mockingly, elbowing Peter in the ribs as he walks past. He winks at me. 'Rese. See you at rehearsal, later?'

I nod. Brad barely notices. He's already turned his attention to Melody, even though he knows trying to use his charm on her is about as worthwhile as trying to kick a goal from the defensive 50.

Peter's ears are pink. 'The blokes call me Johnno,' he whispers.

'Oh, do they?' I raise an eyebrow.

When the footy boys are out of earshot, I whisper, 'You enjoying hanging out with them? Melody says you don't go to the lunch spot at all anymore.'

'Neither do you,' Peter counters.

I nod. 'It's fine. It's fine that neither of us do.'

'Thanks for your permission,' Peter snaps. 'I'm happy. Just like Wally wanted. And, you know, he was wrong about, "just be yourself and the footy boys'll like you". Melody was wrong, too. Maybe they just never saw me before. Now they see me. And they like me just fine like this. Sometimes they even call me Casanova.' He does a little head wiggle and a wink. My stomach drops. 'Now, I'm going to get a sausage roll,' he goes on. 'Is that okay or do I need your go-ahead for that, too?'

'Peter—' I begin, but he's shaking his head, moving away.

'Johnno,' he corrects me. 'Call me Johnno.'

'Um, okay,' I croak. My chest feels hollow.

His eyes narrow as he lowers his voice, 'And you know what? I don't actually give a shit about what Wally wanted. He's dead, anyway, so who cares? Hanging from a fucking tree, so who gives a shit about any of it? I know you've got some secret with him that makes you "special", but who gives a shit about whether a dead guy thinks you're special? What matters is *now*. And now, I'm happy. I'm happy hanging out with those guys, yeah. They see me. I've moved on, Resey. You should, too.'

I watch, eyes stinging, as he walks over to the counter. He barely looks at Melody as he orders his lunch and I can see the hurt on her face.

I know it's my fault. I know I'm the one who broke us; even after Wally made the cracks, it was me who made us shatter. But I always had, in the back of my mind, the idea that we'd glue back together when … when I'm ready.

But what if, when I'm ready, our pieces are too scattered? What if, when I'm ready, the others aren't?

I watch as Melody hands Peter his sausage roll and smiles.

She's always so brave. I miss her. I want to tell her that right now.

But I can't leave the door. I have to keep my position, letting people in, ten at a time. And Melody has to bag up the sausage rolls and pasties, putting scoops of ice cream in the milkshakes.

She's not a natural at it like I am. She doesn't take pride in it like I do.

She chats too much to the kids she's serving. I hear her

tell a little Grade Seven boy that if he ever needs to talk about his crush, she'll make a time.

She puts too many slices of tomato in the rolls and not enough cheese. She squirts far too much sauce on the pies. She flirts with the girls and argues with the boys. She is, generally, the worst canteen helper of all time. But that's why I love her.

Melody only cares about the things that matter. She cares about feminism, and LGBT+ rights. She cares about psychology. She cares about her friends.

She doesn't give a shit about sauce-to-pie ratios.

We switch, so I'm frying chips and handing over Paddle Pops.

And, before we know it, the bell is ringing for the end of lunch. I'm stuck serving the last stragglers and Melody's taking off her apron and walking out the door without looking back.

And I feel like it's all falling down around my feet. Everything used to be so solid and sure. A perfect, unbreakable little universe. We lived above the clouds and we were okay because we were so strong and so high.

Just us.

Why the hell did Wally have to fall?

Why did he have to pull us all down with him?

Why can't I stop feeling all this shit?

Why can't I be the good griever, who goes to therapy and leans on her friends and cries?

I look down at the pie in front of me on the counter. Just the right amount of sauce. I am a bloody awesome canteen helper.

But the important stuff?
I don't have a clue.

# CHAPTER THIRTY-EIGHT

It's the last musical practice before the first performance.

Jarrod and Mandy are fighting because Mandy has decided that if Jarrod 'goes through with this', and 'does the stupid kissing show', he's 'so yesterday'.

Jarrod is in chaos. Mandy is refusing to leave the rehearsal space until he makes a decision. Brad is yelling at him to 'dump her, Jazza'.

Brad's new sort-of-girlfriend, chorus-girl Kelsey, is punching him on the arm, telling him not to be so insensitive.

The other footy boys—'Johnno' included—are standing outside, pulling faces at him through the window, as they wait for training to start on the oval.

Mr Lohrey is struggling to maintain any sort of control.

I'm finishing my maths homework while I wait for it all to blow over. I'm a bit behind because of all my adventures with Rhino.

But I'm also struggling to care.

I just keep thinking about that pie in the canteen and how the sauce was perfect.

It doesn't matter.

And maths doesn't matter.

And this musical doesn't matter.

Last night, I dreamed I was running through a wide, open field and when I reached the end of it, panting and broken, there was a tree with a rope hanging from it. Tied to the rope was Wally's guernsey, covered in blood.

And there was a note on the ground, under the rope. But it wasn't the note that Wally left. It was a different note. It was a poem.

*If I had only had a moment more*
*And in that moment you had come*
*And if you had told me then what I meant to you*
*I never would have fallen.*

I woke up, curled in a ball, shaking. And wondering; wondering if he ever knew.

If he really ever knew how important he was to all of us. How important we all were to each other. All of us just us— bright some days, dark the next, but always there.

I think now of Wally and his notebook. I wonder what he wrote in it. Did he write poems, like I do?

I wonder if he wrote about the chook shed or how my lips felt on his.

*I wonder when we'll kiss again.*

'Are you okay, Resey?'

'Hmm?' I look up. Mr Lohrey is standing over me, his frizzy brown hair even more frenzied than usual. Mr Lohrey's hair always reflects his mood. Today it's as anxious as he is.

'Are you okay?' Mr Lohrey rubs at his forehead. 'It's just, you're ...'

He indicates at my maths exercise book. The writing is smudged, the pages are wet. My hand flies to my face.

I'm crying.

'Don't let all of this bother you,' Mr Lohrey says, gently. 'Jarrod has decided to go ahead with the show and it's going to be a cracker. You're doing so well. We're all … in awe of you. So proud of you. And we're all here for you. I hope you know that. You're not alone.'

When I don't answer, Mr Lohrey clears his throat. 'Everyone is going to just love you as Audrey. If I can only get Brad to concentrate more on remembering his lines than slobbering all over that poor girl, I think this is going to be the best show we've done at this school since *Gumshoe*, back in 1997.'

Mr Lohrey puts his hand gently on my shoulder, his face softening again. 'Resey … you know what, scratch what I just said about being proud of you. I mean, I am. We all are, incredibly. But don't let that make you think … you have to do this. Any of this. If you pulled out today, it wouldn't matter. The only thing that matters is that you're okay. We'll still be here for you, we'll still be proud of you, if you did decide you can't do this. If you weren't … okay.'

He looks so uncomfortable saying all those soft, kind things. It makes my heart feel so withered. I don't want him to worry about me. I don't want anyone to worry about me.

'I'm fine,' I tell him, wiping roughly at the tears on my face. 'I promise. But …' I look around the room, at the other kids. Still wondering.

And, suddenly, the room feels too small.

'Can you spare me?' I blurt. 'I mean, would it be okay if I just … wasn't here?'

'Well …' Mr Lohrey hesitates, examining me with a

furrowed brow. 'Well, yes, of course. If you need to leave the show … I said that and I meant it, but—'

It's all I need to hear.

'I'm not leaving the show.' It's true. Despite how meaningless it all feels, I can't run away from this show. Because it did mean something to me once, and I hope it will again, because if I lose hope … if I lose that something to look forward to then …

'I promise I'll be back tomorrow,' I say, hastily gathering up my books. 'And the show will be great. But I just need to … go.'

As I run from the room, feeling all the eyes on me, like so many tiny bee stings, I pull out my phone and scroll through my contacts until I find the one I need; the person I need to help me with this thing I have to do.

'Rhino?' I say when he answers. 'I hope you're not busy because I've decided I'm taking you on an adventure.'

# CHAPTER THIRTY-NINE

The year before I was born they went to Marrakech, to the same ashram where Grandma T had lived and researched.

My dad didn't really want to go. He'd just finished his business degree and had been offered several jobs in town at accountancy firms and two of the banks.

'Jobs can wait,' she said. 'Boring, adult responsibilities can wait. Life won't wait. We have to grab it now.'

She asked Auntie Kath to go, too, but she was in the middle of her final honours year at the art school and couldn't leave.

'I wish I'd taken that adventure with them,' she says now. She stares out the window, when she says it: remembering and regretting.

They went to a retreat in the hills near the High Atlas Mountains. They did yoga and cooked organic food. They meditated by the river and chanted every morning at daybreak.

They went on day trips to the souk, to see snake charmers and spice stalls, with their undulating hills of red and yellow and green. She ate saffron for the first time, and said she wanted to start a farm back home.

They saw porcupines and cheetahs, lions and mongoose. She wondered, aloud, if they'd see a tiger—her favourite animal—and was told there were no tigers in Morocco. She'd have to go to India for that.

'Next year,' she declared, 'we'll go to India and we'll see a tiger.'

As the sun set, they drank fragrant tea and learned the Arabic names of the constellations. My dad held her hand and kissed her neck beneath a sky that seemed so much bigger than the sky of our small town.

And they talked about leaving; about running away. My dad was reluctant, but she was bursting with the prospect of a life of adventure. That was what she was made for. A life of nights like this, under a foreign sky, her head on the shoulder of the man she loved.

'And then she came home with you in her belly.'

She'd never meant to get pregnant. She'd never thought of kids at all. Her life was boundless, and that's exactly the life designed for someone like her. But on those hills, by that river, below that magic sky, on the other side of the world, she lost herself.

She found out a month after they came home.

Everyone told her that now Marrakech would be her last adventure.

Everyone, apart from Auntie Kath, who told her that I would be her greatest adventure yet.

Her Wonderland.

Mum cried for a week.

'But she must have wanted me,' I say to Auntie Kath. 'At some point she must have wanted me. Otherwise, she would have ...' The thought is sharp and scraping in my head. 'Otherwise, she would have given me up. Or ... or got rid of me.'

My stomach lurches as I say it.

'Always heading off in the wrong direction,' Grandma T always says.

My mum could have run then. Before I was born. She could have made the choice that meant I never was.

A choice that meant I'd never have met Wally. Or, maybe, that I'd now be in the place where he is—a place of nothing.

'She must have thought, at some point, that she wanted a baby?' I prompt Auntie Kath.

Auntie Kath nods, her eyes shining. 'Yes, of course, Tiger. She wanted you to live, especially after all those times when it looked like you wouldn't. She wanted you to hold on. She wanted you to be in the world. She made the decision that she was going to have you and, while you were still inside her, she thought she could do it. She did love you, Tiger. More than the sky.'

A tear rolls down my auntie's beautiful face, and I feel one on mine, as well. I hug her and, like always, I'm so grateful for her. I'm grateful for her kind of love. One that's bigger than the sky, but solid, too. One that feels like home.

The doorbell rings. Rhino.

'I'll be back soon,' I tell Auntie Kath.

'Be safe,' she says. 'Don't run too far away. Always come back to me.'

I let myself stop for a moment to hold her. She pulls away and looks into my eyes. Hers are shining. 'Please never think that because your mother left, you aren't loved. Or special.

Or incredible. You are all those things to me. You are my heart, Tiger. You are my greatest adventure. Please promise me that you won't leave me.'

'I promise,' I whisper, my voice shuddering, cracking. 'I won't ever run too far away from you. You are my home.'

# CHAPTER FORTY

We buy two tickets for the Redline bus.

Rhino offers to drive to 'wherever', but the bus feels important. It's part of this story.

The Redline is full of old people, tourists and the boarder kids from our school.

And other lost people like us.

We stash our bags in the overhead racks and take our seats, halfway between the front and back.

And, finally, Rhino asks, 'Where are we going?'

'Launceston.'

'Launceston,' he repeats. 'That's pretty far away, Tiger.'

'It could have been Marrakech,' I point out. 'Launceston is closer.'

He looks at his watch. 'We'll get there when the elves come out. Cool.' He grins. 'I would run away with you!'

'You know there's no bus back tonight,' I tell him. 'The next one isn't until six tomorrow morning. I'll take that one. It'll get me back in time for school. But there's still time for you to pike out. Go back to your house and watch Netflix or something. Go over to your girlfriend's house and—'

'No,' Rhino says, firmly. 'I'm coming on this adventure

with you, Tiger. I'm just wondering where we'll sleep tonight.'

I gesture around me as the bus pulls out onto Mount Street. 'Under the stars ...'

'Tiger, it's August. In Tasmania. I'm all for adventure, but I'm just not so sure I'm up for frostbite. And you definitely can't sing and dance in the school musical tomorrow if they have to hack your frozen legs off.'

'Fair point.' I shrug. 'So we'll find a hotel. I have plenty of money saved up. No big deal.'

'Um ...' Rhino's voice cracks. 'A hotel room?'

I dig him in the ribs with my elbow. 'Separate beds, Rhino. Don't worry. Separate rooms, if that would make you feel more comfortable, or if it would bother your girlfriend.' More seriously, I ask, 'She'll be okay with this, won't she? You going to Launceston with me for the night?'

Rhino nods. 'It's fine. And … just separate beds will be fine if ... I mean ...' He runs his hand through his long dark hair. 'Just whatever is fine. You're controlling the purse strings, little Bayside Tiger. You're in charge.'

'Bayside Tiger? Nineties reference?'

Rhino puffs out his cheeks. 'You're about to break my heart by telling me you never watched *Saved by the Bell*, aren't you?'

''Fraid so.'

'There is absolutely no hope for you, Tiger Geeves.'

We travel in silence for a little while, until we pull up by the beach in Penguin.

The sky is beginning to turn pink already. It will be witch-cat-black by the time we get to the Gorge. But I don't mind. Somehow, it feels more daring doing this at night-time.

Next to me, Rhino clears his throat. 'So, Tiges. How's tricks?'

'Chillin'. Killin',' I say, quickly, turning to smile at him.

His caterpillar eyebrows bunch up. 'Really?'

'Truly-ruly. Why so serious, Rhino?'

'Just doing my civic duty. Checking you're not all … Tiger, I just feel like I should ask, you know? God, let me just care.' His jaw tenses and when he talks again it's through his teeth. 'Are. You. Okay?'

Goosebumps prickle on my arms. 'Totally fine,' I snap. 'I mean, my best friend—and, you know, I think the only boy I ever loved, just died. And it was my fault. Because he tried to tell me and I didn't listen. So yeah, I'm awesome. What do you want from me?'

Rhino's face empties. 'Did he love you back?'

'It felt like he did when he kissed me.'

Rhino turns away.

There's silence from Ulverstone to Devonport.

When we stop at the Devonport terminal I can't take it any longer. 'Rhino, you could get off now, you know. I'm pretty sure that bus over there goes back home. I'll pay for your ticket. You don't have to come with me.'

Rhino continues to look out the window at the new passengers streaming from the waiting lounge towards the bus.

Finally, he turns around. 'Why did the tiger lose at poker?'

A relieved giggle escapes. 'I dunno, Rhino. Why did the tiger lose at poker?'

'Because he was playing with a cheetah.'

I know now that everything is going to be okay. Rhino is staying. The adventure continues.

# CHAPTER FORTY-ONE

The Gorge at night-time is as frightening as it is beautiful. Everything shimmers as if it's made of fairy dust. Every shadow looks like a monster.

It is the Otherwhere.

'I could make the best horror movie here,' he's saying, walking backwards ahead of me. 'Maybe with vampires or … or mutant potoroos!'

'Or a really sinister serial killer lurking in the shadows …'

Rhino stops still. 'Okay, Tiges, that's actually much scarier than vampires and mighty morphin' marsupials. Thanks for that. Now I'm properly scared.'

'I could hold your hand, if you like,' I offer. 'In a purely platonic, just-looking-after-a-mate-so-he-doesn't-get-butchered kind of way.'

'Did you have to say the word "butchered"?' asks Rhino, shivering.

I offer him my hand, and he takes it.

A twig snaps and Rhino cowers. 'You absolute wuss,' I tease.

'Lucky I have you to hold my hand,' he says. His voice is soft. I look over at him. His eyes are searching my face.

Something in my belly twists. It's wrong the way he's

looking at me. It's the way Wally looked at me, in the chook shed.

And I get a sinking feeling, like I've overstepped some line into a place where the ground is shaky.

But he has a girlfriend. It's okay.

'Come on,' I say. 'Let's finish this walk. I'm getting cold and hungry.'

'But it's so nice out here with all the potential for being butchered,' Rhino says, as he jogs to keep up with me.

'It is nice,' I agree, dragon-breathing again. 'It's amazing. The stars. The water down there, all shimmery. The little animal eyes peeping out from the ferns. It's incredible. I'm so glad we came.'

'So am I.'

There's still something off about Rhino's voice. I decide to ignore it. 'So, since we're here, in the Tasmanian wilderness, maybe you should tell me a Tasmanian tiger joke,' I suggest.

'Therese—'

The sound of my name—my actual name—makes me freeze. Rhino has never called me that before. He's never even called me Resey.

I let go of his hand. 'Why'd you call me that?'

His eyes are all soft again.

'You've gone serious again,' I accuse.

'Sometimes … it's necessary,' he says. He looks like he's shaking. Or maybe I'm shaking.

'I don't believe you're okay,' he says, softly.

'Rhino,' I say, my voice lowered in warning.

'I don't know how you could be okay. Losing someone you … loved, like that. Losing such a close friend. I mean, if I lost you ... I'm ... worried about losing you, Tiger. You said he tried to tell you and you didn't ... Maybe your friends are right, Tiger. Maybe you should be talking to someone—'

'Oh, not you too!' I yell. 'What the hell do you think I'm going to do?'

'I don't—'

I gesture at the trees. 'Am I going to take a rope and tie it around my neck and climb up that trunk and fix the rope to a branch and jump and snap my neck?'

'Tiger ...'

'Am I going to climb up to that bridge?' My voice is growing louder. I'm pacing. I need to move; need to yell and get all of this out of me. 'Am I going to leap into the water; crack my head on the rocks; bleed to death in the middle of all this?'

I'm running now. I'm a girl, in the moonlight, running towards the water. I'm a girl who wishes she could run forever, but feels like, instead, she might fall.

'Why would I do that?' I roar, as I run. 'Why would I? I'm Therese Geeves. I'm perfect. I'm golden. Just because my own parents didn't love me enough to stay; just because my best friend didn't love me enough to stay, even after we kissed. Why the hell would I do anything?'

I'm at the water's edge now. The cold night air enters my mouth, my throat, in gulping, jagged, icy shards. There's not enough room in my lungs and my heart beats so fast, so fast, so fast, and it's going to stop. A heart can't beat that fast and not stop. A girl can't feel like this and not stop.

*'Tiger! Stop!'*

But I won't. I won't stop. I can't stop. I've come this far

and the water is so nice on my feet, my thighs, my waist. It feels cold. It feels *real*. I gasp, and then I cry—finally, I cry. I sob and I wail and it feels so awful, but so wonderful.

'Tiger!'

And I fall.

I plunge beneath the water's surface.

And everything is darkness.

And it's so nice to just fall.

But then his arms are around me and they push the air from my lungs and I swallow so much water and it tastes of dirt and death.

And he is dragging me back to life.

We lie panting on the rocky ground of the basin.

'Fuck, Tiger,' he murmurs.

He moves away from me and comes back with a jacket. He wraps it around my shoulders. My arms are shivering. My skin feels blue.

'Are you okay?' he asks.

'Dumb qu-question,' I manage, around my chattering teeth.

'You scared me.'

It's an accusation and it's angry.

I don't reply; can't reply. So Rhino continues quickly, words pouring from his mouth like a waterfall. 'You know how you felt about Wally? Well, that's how I feel about you, and you know how you felt when he died? Well, that's how I'd feel if you died, and that's absolutely devastated. So just … don't do stuff like that, Tiger. Ever again. Just, please, be okay. Please be okay. Please.'

There is a long silence between us. All the sounds of the

night in the Gorge fill it and they sound like a symphony.

And they sound … beautiful.

And this whole place is beautiful.

And for a moment, just then, as I sit, shuddering and wet beneath Rhino's coat, I feel alive. *Properly alive.* And like life might be bizarrely beautiful, too.

But I am cold. And I am wet. And I am starving. And I can't sit here any longer or I think I might freeze in this spot forever.

'I will be okay. I—'

'Promise. You have to promise.'

His eyes scan my face. His neck is so tight, I can see the veins pressed against the skin.

'I promise. But –'

'No "buts".'

'But,' I say, more firmly, 'I am bloody cold. And I am very, very hungry.'

Rhino's face suddenly breaks into a big, beautiful grin.

'We could go to Morty's,' I suggest. 'They do kebabs there if you want one. I, on the other hand, could … murder a curry.'

To my relief, Rhino laughs. 'You're evil, Tiger.'

'You …' I begin to walk more quickly, 'are paying for dinner, if I beat you to the exit!'

I stand, shakily. My feet squelch when I take a step. But I need to run again. This time, though, in the right direction.

I break into a sprint.

'You're on!' Rhino cries.

We race, bellowing, around the windy track towards the first basin, scaring the life out of the night creatures as we do it.

And I think: this is it.

*This is life.*

This is adventure.

Even though I'm soaked to the skin and will possibly have the flu tomorrow.

Even though I just completely lost the plot in the middle of the Cataract Gorge.

I am okay.

But even as I run and laugh, I know it needs to end. Not with running into a river.

With something that leads to happiness. With something that leads to life.

# CHAPTER FORTY-TWO

Things feel lighter after that between Rhino and me. We go to the food hall and both change in the toilets into warm, dry clothes. Rhino orders pasta and convinces me to have a curry pie. I ring Auntie Kath to check in; he calls his parents to do the same. Later we go to our hotel suite—with separate rooms—and take huge delight in being naughty, eating four-dollar Mars Bars from the minibar. And then we watch *Doctor Who* before going to our separate beds.

My phone alarm wakes us the next morning at five o'clock. We're back, grumbling, on the bus by six.

I feel utterly wrecked but happy. I'm glad I had the adventure. I'm glad I had it with Rhino.

But I'm glad even more that I'm going home.

I didn't dream of Wally—at all—in the hotel room.

But when I close my eyes on the bus it's still only him inside me.

'Tell me a joke,' I say to Rhino.

'Too tired. Too hungry. *Too, too, too,*' Rhino moans.

'We'll get brekkie together when we get home,' I offer. 'My shout.'

'I want hotcakes,' Rhino says, petulantly. 'When I feel

this gross, nothing else will do.'

I wrinkle my nose. 'I was thinking heirloom tomato bruschetta, with sweetcorn and avocado cream ...'

'Hipster,' Rhino laughs.

'Bogan,' I retort.

We pull into our town. It's where Wally lived and where he died and where I was born and where I was left. It's my story. It's my home.

Auntie Kath is here and Grandma T.

The bus drives along the road by the beach and I watch as a family runs along the sand with a big golden retriever. Something inside me aches a bit.

I realise that Rhino is talking to me.

'Sorry, Rhino. I was miles away.'

'Just wondering if you're nervous about tonight?' Rhino rakes his hand through his un-brushed, crow-feather hair, and pulls a rubber band around it. 'The first performance?'

I think hard about his question. If he'd asked me a couple of weeks ago, I would have replied that I was ridiculously nervous. It's my first lead role; half the school, and much of the town, will be there watching me. The footy boys will be there watching me.

And Mel and Roz and Peter and Rhino and Flo.

Wally would've been there.

But now?

Wally is dead and I'm dressing up in high heels, with a blonde wig, and being eaten by a green foam plant.

But ... there is still something there. I still want this. I still want to be an actor. My stomach knots and I realise that I am actually a bit nervous. Maybe I'm still breathing after all.

'It will be fine,' is all I say to Rhino.

We're at the terminal now. I stand and pull my bag from the overhead compartment.

I feel Rhino's hand on my arm. 'Hey, it means a lot to me that you wanted me there on this adventure with you.'

'It means heaps to me that you came. And I'm sorry about freaking out at the Gorge. I was just being—'

'Normal.' Rhino smiles. 'You were just being exactly how someone should be after what's happened. It's all good. Anything you do is all good with me.'

I don't know what to say to that, so instead I ask, 'How's tricks, Rhino?'

I expect him to laugh, but he shakes his head, and walks ahead of me out of the bus. I follow him. 'What was that about?' I ask when I join him on the street.

'Nothing ...' His smile is forced. 'I'm just chillin' and killin' for some breakfast, that's all. But not McDonald's, okay? We'll go to The Chapel. Artisan, fair-trade, distressed kale and tampered-with goji berries it is.'

'You won't regret it,' I say. 'Stuart makes the best cold-drip coffee—'

'As long as you don't go Full Hipsterzilla and order the kombucha.'

'Promise. And ... you know, we could compromise. Do both. The Chapel first, then Banjo's for breakfast pies?'

'Deal,' he says. 'And crappy cappuccinos with too many sugars.'

'And date scones ...' I finish, my tummy grumbling.

'And then ... I have to put on my tie and knee socks and get to school,' Rhino says. 'And so do you.'

'Adventure officially ended,' I sigh, hoisting my bag over my shoulder.

'Only this one. We'll have many more adventures together, I promise, Tiger. To the Otherwhere and Everywhere. But even great adventurers must stop for breakfast.'

I want to look like I'm sure, but I can't imagine more adventures with Rhino. This was the last one.

I look up to the sky. I'm home.

*Are you watching me, Wally?* I think. *I'm still here.*

Dear Mum,

Tonight there will be lights on me.

Tonight people will clap for me.

Tonight people will see me and know I'm good.

Not you, though.

Never you.

But, I think, that's okay.

I think Wally will be watching.

# CHAPTER FORTY-THREE

Mr Lohrey hands me a bunch of flowers. 'We especially want to thank you, Tiger, for your commitment to this show. You are such a strong young woman and you put on an incredible performance tonight. It's enough to make me forgive you for your disappearing act yesterday ...' He raises an eyebrow, and smiles at me, wryly.

I look at my feet, still in my black patent 'Audrey' high heels. I'm dying to kick them off and get my Volleys on.

'I really am sorry about that,' I say to Mr Lohrey. It's about the tenth time I've apologised, but he doesn't seem mad. He seems to understand.

'Never mind,' he says. 'That's not important now. What's important is all your hard work and the brilliant job you did tonight. Everybody give Tiger a round of applause.'

There are claps and whistles. Jarrod even kisses me on the cheek. Across the theatre, I see Mandy, glowering. They're still together but only by a thread.

We've still got two performances to go, but everyone is already feeling relieved. Tonight we got two standing ovations. Tomorrow and Sunday will be fine.

My cheer squad are all here: Roz, Melody, Peter, Rhino,

Flo, Lexi, Grandma T, Granda Craig and Auntie Kath. They whooped and whistled whenever I came on stage. Peter yelled out, 'Go you good thing, Resey!' after I sang 'Somewhere That's Green'. He sat with his new girlfriend, a Grade Nine footy fan called Ella. She seems awesome and like the sort of girl who takes no shit from anyone. And, with her, the bullshit seems actually, finally gone. It was only ever an act. And maybe it worked for a while. He got in with the footy jocks just like he always wanted. But it looks like that's lost its shine. That or he likes Ella more.

Or he just finally realised that Wally was right. Being someone you're not sucks. And it doesn't ever make you happy in the long run. So Peter's lost that arsehole façade. And he's found someone to be with, who likes him the way we always knew he was deep inside. I'm happy for him.

I'm happy that he came, and Melody and Roz too. But even if it means they forgive me, I can't leave it at that. I can't just let this whole thing disappear. I'm here now. *For good.*

Because I know I might be like her in so many ways, but I'm different from her in so many ways, too. We are both many pieces, but the pieces of me fit together differently from the way hers fit. I'm not a slippery baby bird. I'm a Tiger with claws that hang on.

She ran. Wally fell. I'm here.

On my desk at home there is a card from Brisbane.

*So proud of you, Therese,* it says. *Wish we could have been there. Good luck. I'm sure you will be wonderful.*

They can't wish to be here too strongly. Otherwise, they would be.

The people who matter are here.

Even Wally. He is here. I felt him when I was on stage. And I did feel golden. For the first time, I felt like he was telling the truth.

After Mr Lohrey is finished with us, Melody and Roz rush to hug me.

'I'm sorry, guys,' I whisper in their ears.

Melody shakes her head. 'Not now,' she says. 'No talking now. Enjoy your moment.' More arm squeezes and they're waving goodbye.

Peter fills the empty space, claps me on the arm. 'Well done, Resey. You were awesome up there.'

'Aww, shucks.' My grin fades. I glare at my feet. 'Hey, um, I know … I know you must be so angry at me. Because you were hurting and stuff, and I wasn't there for you like I should have been. And I didn't talk to you like I should have. And I wanted to say … I'm sure he thought you were golden, too.'

Peter inclines his head. 'Nah, mate. I'm glad he didn't. Too much pressure being golden. Easier—more fun—being just … normal. You can get up to all sorts of mischief if you're not all gold and glowing.' He flashes me a wicked grin, then it slides from his face. 'But, look, you were there for me, Resey, when I needed you to be. At the wake, in the bathroom. That's when I needed you and you were there. I'm the one who hasn't been there for you. I should be saying sorry. I was rude to you the other day and we both … both of us are hurting. We should look after each other, not fight.'

I nod. My chest feels less tight now. My heart feels a bit fuller. 'I'm so glad you came,' I say. 'Thank you so much for being here and cheering and stuff.'

'No worries,' he says. 'You can cheer for me next weekend when I'm playing against North Hobart.'

My mouth drops open. 'What? Peter—I mean Johnno—seriously? I didn't think you could play for the team unless you got picked at the start of the season?'

Peter shrugs. 'Let's just call it a present from Wally.'

And then I realise: the reason there's a space on the team.

Peter is silent, his eyes fixed on mine. Waiting. Waiting, I guess, for me to say it's okay.

'I'm proud of you,' I tell him. 'I bet Wally is, too.'

Peter smiles. Nods. Grateful.

Then I see Ella, hovering by the door. She lifts her hand to wave and I wave back. Peter looks like he's won the lottery.

'Not going off to cog around town with Brad and Pedda in Simmo's Cordia?' I ask, raising an eyebrow.

Peter puffs out his cheeks. 'Nah, mate,' he says, quietly. He leans in. 'Between you and me, Rese, those guys are arseholes.'

Auntie Kath comes up next and gives me a huge, squeezing hug. 'Tiges, I am so … so … stuffed full of pride,' she says, pulling back. There are tears in her eyes. 'I'm coming back tomorrow night. And Sunday. I could watch you sing and dance all day. You're astonishingly wonderful.'

'Now, now,' I say. 'You'll give me a big head, Auntie Kath.'

'And I made you these.' Auntie Kath looks bashful as she passes over our biscuit tin. 'To say congratulations. They're meant to be football-shaped cookies. I got the idea from Nerdy Nummies on YouTube. The icing's a bit wonky, but I made them all by myself.'

'Now I'm pride-stuffed,' I say, laughing. 'Well done, you.'

'And, uh …' Auntie Kath's forehead crinkles. 'Tiger, I

didn't want to tell you this before the performance, but as I was leaving, I got a phone call. From Queensland. She—'

'Can we talk about it later?' I ask. My heart is jittering.

'Of course,' Auntie Kath says, quietly.

We're joined then by Lexi, who gives me a hug and ruffles my hair. She's wearing a Sampa the Great tee-shirt, skinny green jeans and holding a plastic container of her own. Dumplings. They smell like heaven. 'You were fabulous up there, little Resey-girl,' she says. 'You will be a famous movie star one day.'

'Thanks, Lexi,' I say, blushing.

'You must come over to our place soon, before Hollywood snatches you away!' She lowers her voice. 'Melody would like you to. She misses you. She might pretend to be strong and invincible my girl, but inside she's soft like jelly. And she says you're still not talking about Nick Wallace.' She raises an eyebrow, looking for a moment exactly like her daughter.

I shake my head. 'Soon, though,' I say.

'I've been telling Mellie to let you come to it in your own time,' Lexi says, tutting and shaking her head. 'My daughter is a piranha. A soft jelly piranha.'

I laugh. 'Yes, she is. In a good way, though.'

'And, in the meantime, I made you dumplings and—' Lexi hands over a USB stick. 'Mp3. Of all my favourite sad music and angry music and happy music. They are all in files with these labels. Melody and I might talk all the time, analyse everything to death, but I only do that with Mellie because it's what she needs. You are maybe different. You work through things differently. Until you are ready to talk, you listen to this music—whatever mood you need. Maybe it will help just as much.'

'Thank you, Lexi,' I say, and give her another hug.

'And you will come over soon! I'll make you a special banquet. You deserve it.'

Grandma T is next. She kisses me on the forehead. 'My tiny little girl,' she whispers. 'So grown up. Please promise me you'll come to the farm soon and look for elves in the chook shed. I don't think I could take it if you thought you were too old for that.'

'Never too old,' I say, and I promise to visit soon.

I will visit soon.

I'll visit the elves. I'll visit Wally, too. I'll talk to him. I'll tell him what he's missing out on. But I won't tell him angrily. I'm not angry anymore. Not really. I know now what it feels like to just want to run or fall or escape. I wish he'd known there could be another way. I wish he knew things could get better. But I'm not angry. Just sad.

I can't feel too sad, though, when I see Flo and Rhino approaching. My friends. My laughter.

They come up to me dancing choreographed Spice Girls moves. It's brilliant, and so totally them.

'I can't stay,' Flo says, after twirling me around. 'I have to go to work. I got called in. Um, Jamie was, like, really desperate and—' I can't help but notice there's a flush to Flo's cheeks when she says his name.

I incline my head to one side. 'Jamie, hey?'

'Don't even,' Flo growls. 'I'll tell you about it on Tuesday, okay?' She can't stop a grin from spreading over her face.

Rhino and I exchange freaked-out looks.

'Anyway, I just wanted to say you were amazing,' says

Flo. 'And I'm glad. Really glad that you seem to be doing well. You're doing much better than I did, after my nan died.'

'What do you mean?' I ask, confused.

'I mean I bottled it all up, like I said, and then had a mega meltdown in the middle of the school cafeteria. I needed to talk, I guess, in the end. But if talking doesn't do the job for you, then … whatever works. I'm just glad you're doing okay, because I think you're awesome, comrade.'

'Yeah, you too.' Flo gives me a big hug and a kiss on the cheek. 'But I'm going to talk. No meltdowns here.'

'Glad, comrade. Laters,' she says.

'Give the Jamienator our regards,' Rhino says.

'I'll give him a big kiss for you!' Flo calls out and then claps a hand over her mouth and giggles. She turns on her heel and runs away before we can say anything else.

'I think I can feel my taco coming back up,' Rhino says, shaking his head. 'Florence and the Machine. Who'da thunk it.' He turns to me. 'Anyway, to change the subject— because it makes me feel nauseous to even think of that abomination—well done, Tiger.' He holds out a hand for me to shake. 'Sterling job.'

'Thanks, Rhino,' I say. 'But you know, I was really just chillin' up there …'

'Killin' it more like,' he says, grinning. But then he looks more serious; looks away at something behind my shoulder. 'And, hey, I was just wondering what you're up to now. You know, if you're free … I was wondering if maybe, you and me …' He scrunches up his face and growls. 'Shit, Therese. I'm trying to ask you out.'

My heart stops. 'Rhino …' I begin, too full of bemusement

to say much more than his name.

'There's no girlfriend,' he blurts. 'I lied. Haha! I am an international man of mystery. There's only you. And I know that ... well, you and Wally, but ...'

I'm nodding. He sees me nod. He sees my eyes. He knows. Puffs his cheeks. 'Yeah, well, I'll be here, you know, if ...' He shakes his head. 'Have I got a chance, Tiges? Straight up?'

And I want to tell him, 'Yes, of course!' I want to see him smile. I want to give him hope.

But Rhino always felt like running. I don't want to do that anymore.

And when I close my eyes, all I can see is Wally.

*Still.*

And I know it won't always be that way. It will get better. I will survive, move on, dream about something other than him. I will fall in love again one day but ...

Not yet.

'Can we at least still be friends forever, despite the humiliation to which I have just subjected myself? Because, you know, then I can sing that song ...' His voice goes up an octave as he hums the hit tune by Vitamin C. The relief is intense.

'Definitely! Definitely friends forever, Rhino. No way I want to miss out on the rest of your pie odyssey. But, please, stop it with that awful song.'

Rhino gives me a little bow. 'Cool. Well, take care of you, Tiger G.'

His smile is sad. I hope he'll be okay. As he backs away, he says, 'What's the silliest name you can give a tiger? Spot!' And then he's gone.

I think he'll be okay.

# CHAPTER FORTY-FOUR

I sit on my bedroom floor, my back against the bed. I'm holding Wally's guernsey. It doesn't feel like a monster anymore.

The Streets is playing on my computer—one of Lexi's Mp3s. It's all loss and torture.

A mug of Milo and the footy biscuits are sitting on the floor beside me.

The biscuits are a bit burned, but that's not why I'm not eating them. I'm not eating Lexi's dumplings, either.

I want to know what's written inside the guernsey—the other message that Wally told me about. But, at the same time, I really don't.

I'm scared.

'I have to do this,' I whisper to myself. 'I'm sick of running.'

My mum ran. My dad ran. Wally fell. I don't want to be like them. I want to be like Auntie Kath and Grandma T. I want to stay and face this.

I press the guernsey to my face.

It doesn't smell like him. It smells of fabric softener and dust. I run my fingers over the darning.

I turn it inside out.

My heart feels more exposed than it ever has before.

Dear Mum,
I'm frightened.

# CHAPTER FORTY-FIVE

Pinned to the inside of Wally's guernsey is a photograph and a folded piece of paper.

The photograph is of us: Wally, me, Peter, Melody and Roz. It wasn't taken on a special occasion. We are just sitting at the lunch spot in our school uniforms. I'm holding half a chocolate chip biscuit and Wally has the other half. Melody's mouth is full of pork bun and Roz is laughing at her. Peter is poking out his tongue at the person holding the camera.

I can't even remember who took the photo. Who would we have asked?

There was only us. The five of us. We were everything.

I open the piece of paper. It's a short note, written in Wally's familiar handwriting. It's addressed to us.

I turn the photo over and my breath catches in my throat.

My fingers trace the words, in his funny, scrawly handwriting.

*What's important is this photo.*

*Us.*

*We are the brightest, the most burning, a song and a poem and I—*

*Give it to you.*

*The photo.*

*Us.*

*Because I want to be with you, always.*
*I wish I could be but I can't.*
*Please don't hate me for that.*
*The four of you are my everything; more important than anything.*
*You're all enough. You're all perfect.*
*All golden. But not the solid kind of golden. The sort that breaks;*
*Splinters;*
*Cracks.*
*The sort that lets the light in.*
*The sort that isn't fixed but can be moulded into anything.*
*I'll watch you always now; watch you changing; becoming brilliant.*
*I'll make sure you're happy.*
*Stay exactly how you are because exactly how you are is the best thing there is.*
*And remember*
*What's important is this photo.*
*Us.*
*You.*
*You are the brightest, the most burning, a song and a poem and you*
*Must constantly change;*
*Must never change.*
*Must fall.*
*Must fly.*
*Must live,*
*For me.*

There's a rustling sound outside my bedroom window. I look through the tears at the sunset sky. My breath catches in my throat. Soaring upwards towards the clouds is the shape of a sparrowhawk.

'Wally,' I whisper.

# CHAPTER FORTY-SIX

Auntie Kath is standing at my bedroom door.

When I look up, she says, quietly, 'Can I come in?'

I nod. I pass her the photo and turn it over to show her the note. She reads in silence. When she's finished she looks at me and says, 'Do you want me to ring Lexi and tell her to send Melody over?'

I nod. 'And Roz and Peter. Please.'

'Lexi will be happy,' Auntie Kath says. 'She's called three times this week already to ask after you. She kept talking about some guy called Urthboy and pork buns ...'

I laugh, despite myself, and gesture at the stereo. A different hip hop singer, called Illy, is singing a sad song about chasing memories.

I press a button on my laptop and the music changes to a bouncy song by Drapht. 'The sad stuff helped,' I say. 'But I need some happy music now. And I need my friends.'

Fifteen minutes later, Melody pokes her head around my bedroom door. She sits down next to me.

'Melody, I am so bloody—' I begin. I will fix this now.

'Shut up, Resey,' she growls. 'No talking. None of it matters, okay?'

'But I'm—'

'I said, shut up, or I'll do some major kung fu on your butt, okay?'

I nod and smile.

Sometimes things fix themselves.

'Now come here.' Melody's chin trembles. 'Crap. I told myself I wasn't going to cry.'

'Cry,' I say. 'Cry all you want and talk all you want. I'm here. I'll listen.'

I wrap my best friend in my arms and then we sit together, rocking and crying, until we hear Peter's voice. 'Bloody hell.'

Roz finds us, half an hour later, lying on my bedroom floor, bellies full of biscuits and cake, laughing over stories about Wally.

She joins us and picks a footy biscuit up from the plate. 'These are burned,' she says. 'Auntie Kath?'

'She tried,' I say.

Roz shrugs. 'I'm starving. I'll give it a go. Hey, remember when we were making rocky road in home economics, and Wally burned the chocolate? It was all lumpy and weird, but he tried some and it tasted awesome so we ate it all anyway.'

'Yes!' Peter smacks his head. 'I forgot about that. We were going to make it a "thing" and market it as "Wally Wonka's Weirdly Wonderful Wocolate".'

'*Wocolate!* I remember wocolate!' I cry. 'Hey! We should make some wocolate!'

And so we go to the kitchen and I find a block of Anvers Milk Fortunato. It's Kath's special, expensive treat, so usually, I leave it alone, but I think—in this case—I'm going to make an exception. Wocolate deserves to be made with quality ingredients. While I'm breaking the heavy block into smaller pieces, Peter gets a saucepan, and Melody and Roz find spoons and butter.

'JC would love wocolate,' Melody sighs, staring into the fridge with a giddy grin on her face.

'You love her, don't you?' I ask.

Melody nods. 'It's a beautiful misery.'

'I thought feminists didn't believe in love.' Peter raises an eyebrow.

'You have a fundamentally flawed conception of what feminism is,' Melody says. 'I'm very hopeful that Ella will help fix that. I've been talking to her a lot about intersectional feminism. She's deeply interested in the work of Nnedi Okorafor—did you know that your girlfriend reads feminist sci-fi? But, going back to your theory about feminists rejecting love, actually, Gloria Steinem says that being in a relationship is being limitless, not limited. And, furthermore—'

'All right! All right! Enough, Germaine Greer.'

'Oh, no,' Melody says, darkly. 'Don't get me started on her.'

Peter ignores her. '—Can we make some bloody wocolate already? Geez!'

'But don't you want to hear about—'

'I loved Wally!' I interrupt them, my eyes never leaving my fingertips. 'And he loved me. He kissed me. That's the secret memory he talked about.'

My friends stop their bickering immediately. They drop their cooking tools and surround me; envelope me. And I cry until I feel emptied.

'I knew he loved you,' Peter says. 'I always knew. He told

me back in Grade Seven. He made me promise not to tell. He even wrote poems about you. They weren't bad.'

In that moment, I wish away years. I wish I could fly back to the past and *know*.

But it's not Peter's fault. And there's nothing either of us can say now, except, *'I wish …'*

We say it at the same time. Neither of us finish the sentence because we both know what the end would be.

'I'm so sorry,' Melody says, in a choked, small voice. 'I told you that you should wait …'

'Never mind,' I say, because it's what Grandma T said when I was a little girl, whenever I got sad. And because it isn't Melody's fault, either. 'Never mind.'

And then, after a while of us hugging and crying and healing, I wipe my eyes. 'Right, then. Wocolate.'

When Auntie Kath comes in from a sculpture-material-finding expedition outside, the room is filled with smoke and the four of us are on the floor with chocolate on our chins.

'Can I join you?' Auntie Kath asks.

'Of course!' I say. 'I used your chocolate, after all!'

'I am not even close to being mad.'

Auntie Kath slides down the floor. She sticks her finger into the pot of chocolate and boops me on the nose.

I boop her back.

A booping war begins between all of us.

And I feel happy in that silly moment, with four of the people I love the most.

Knowing that Wally is here with us still.

And will always be.

# CHAPTER FORTY-SEVEN

Auntie Kath sits across from me, pretending to read an art magazine.

I'm staring at the phone.

My box is on the floor beside us. It's empty and the contents are in Auntie Kath's 'Not Just Books' shopper bag, ready to be sent on Tuesday. We always send my memories on a Tuesday.

I wanted her to know that I was having a great life, too, while she had adventures.

I could do all the things.

Be all the things.

And, I thought, if I told her about all that I did and all that I was, packaging it all up into a box, and then an envelope, she'd know I was worth coming home to.

And now, she has finally come home. Only, not to me.

*Marrakech, Goa, Nepal, South Korea, Mongolia, Cuba, South Africa, Turkey, Norway, Finland, Iceland, Egypt, Peru, Scotland ...*

These were all the places we sent my memories too. Every time she moved, we'd get an email, with the subject line, 'Mailing Address'. And the only text in the email was the name of the place where she was living for the next little while; the place where we were to send my memories.

*California, Zimbabwe, Dublin, Minsk, Alberta, New Caledonia, Papua New Guinea, Denpasar, Mexico City, Prague ...*

And the next time we went to the post office, on Tuesday, we'd write that address on the front of the envelope.

Finally, six months ago, the email said:

*5 Lily Avenue*
*Ascot QLD 4007*

My dad's address.

She'd stopped.

I don't know if going to Queensland is her running in the right direction or the wrong one. In his letter, my dad only said that she was living with him and she'd like it very much if we could talk sometime. When I replied I didn't mention her. I didn't say I'd call. I just sent off my memories the next Tuesday to my dad's address. And I put it out of my mind.

And she never called me. And she never wrote.

She waited for me to call her.

Until the night of my performance when she rang Auntie Kath.

She knew I wouldn't be home.

Auntie Kath reckons she's nervous and that's why she's waiting for me to make the first move.

I think she's a coward.

Auntie Kath is doing the crossword in her magazine. 'Christina Booth,' I hear her murmur. She still doesn't look up. She knows that this is a decision I need to make.

My fingers brush against the buttons. I know the number by heart. I know the brave thing to do—the tiger-like, hard thing to do—would be to dial it.

But it's been sixteen years since I've heard her voice. And I don't remember the sound of it.

The first voice I remember is Auntie Kath's.

The first arms I remember holding me close, making me feel safe are Auntie Kath's.

The first walk on the beach, first story, first song, first holding-my-hand, first tickle, first joke—all of them are with Auntie Kath.

My mother sat with her hand pressed against the glass for days until they let her hold me. She held me so tightly while tears coated her face.

Then she got sick. They took her away from me, to her own room, where she fought the infection. For weeks she was in the hospital bed, just down the hallway from the nursery.

She didn't ask to see me again. Not once.

'Always heading off in the wrong direction,' Grandma T says.

Every day that she didn't go to see me, Auntie Kath did. She was the one who gave me my first bottle. She was the one who gave me my first bath. She was the one who changed nappies and stroked my little legs and kissed my downy head and held my hand when they gave me my first injections.

My mum never even said goodbye.

After she ran, my dad went to live with Auntie Kath. He tried to be a dad to me. But every time he looked at my face, he saw my mum and he couldn't cope with the pain of it.

And so it was just us two: Auntie Kath and me. And she loved me fiercely. She was the only mother I ever knew.

And she wrote down all my stories.

*Tiger rolled for the first time today.*

*Tiger will only eat banana.*

*Tiger has gone up a clothes size—again! Cue another frantic grow-suit shop!*

*Tiger poked out her tongue!*

*Tiger used twenty nappies today!*

*Tiger took her first step.*

She wrote it all down for the sister who left. She sent my life away in words. And her sister never replied.

And she never called.

Auntie Kath said that she couldn't; that it would hurt her too much to speak to me. That it would make it real, what she'd done. That it would ruin her adventure. But now she is home. The adventure is over. Mum wants to talk but only if I run towards her.

I look down at my box, the contents of it, in the shopper bag. And I think of Wally's message—the photo and the note.

And I think of the people that matter to me: Melody. Roz. Peter. Flo. Lexi. Grandma T. Granda Craig. Rhino.

*Wally.*

And Auntie Kath, who changed my nappies and cuddled me and fed me and clothed me and laughed with me and played with me and baked me burnt, football-shaped biscuits.

'Luke Wagner,' she murmurs. 'And … Kit Hiller! Well, that's an obvious one!'

'I'm not going to call.'

Auntie Kath looks up. She nods. 'Okay,' she says.

She doesn't ask why. She knows.

'Auntie Kath?'

'Tiger.'

'I was thinking … Maybe we don't need to send the stuff,

any more. If that's okay.'

Again she nods. 'I think that's okay, Tiger.'

'And … if it's okay, I think I'm ready to have my session with Mrs Koetsveld. Could you set it up for me, please?'

'Today?'

I shake my head. 'Soon. But not today.'

Auntie Kath nods. 'I'll ring her this morning.'

'What did you have planned for the rest of today?' I ask.

Auntie Kath gestures at her magazine. 'Well … ring Megan. Finish the crossword. Try to bake some banana muffins with banana in them this time. Not much, really. Why? Did you have plans? Did you want to go and see your friends?'

I shake my head. 'I'll see them soon. I was thinking … you and me. You want to go on an adventure?'

Auntie Kath inclines her head to one side. 'Sure, Tiger,' she says. 'Where would you like to go?'

'Anywhere,' I reply. 'As long as it's with you.'

Dear Wally,
Can you see me still?
I'll keep writing to you.
I want you to know I'm okay,
And that I'll always think
You're golden.
I want you to see me down here,
On the ground ...

Dancing.

# ABOUT THE AUTHOR

Kate Gordon grew up in a very booky house, with two librarian parents, in a small town by the sea in Tasmania. She spent her childhood searching for fossils at Fossil Bluff, wondering about the doctor who rode his horse off the cliff at Doctor's Rocks, and eating the best chips in the world at the fish and chip shop at the wharf. She also spent much of her time dreaming about being a writer, and spent many a lunch hour walking around the playground reciting poetry. The other children thought she was a little bit odd. After studying performing arts and realising she was a terrible actor, Kate decided to give in to genetics and study to be a librarian herself. She never stopped writing and, in 2009, with the encouragement of a very nice man called Leigh (who is also her husband), she applied for and won a Varuna fellowship, which led to all sorts of lovely writer things happening.

If you're affected by any of the issues discussed in
*Girl Running, Boy Falling*, please contact:
Lifeline Australia 13 11 14
Beyondblue.org.au